DEFYING *the* DIVA

ALSO BY D. ANNE LOVE

Picture Perfect

Semiprecious

The Secret Prince

The Puppeteer's Apprentice

•

MARGARET K. McELDERRY BOOKS

DEFYING *the* DIVA

D. Anne Love

MARGARET K. McELDERRY BOOKS
New York   London   Toronto   Sydney

Margaret K. McElderry Books
An imprint of Simon & Schuster Children's
Publishing Division
1230 Avenue of the Americas, New York, New York 10020
Book design by Krista Vossen
The text for this book is set in Fairfield.
Manufactured in the United States of America
2 4 6 8 10 9 7 5 3
Library of Congress Cataloging-in-Publication Data
Love, D. Anne.
Defying the diva / D. Anne Love.—1st ed.
p. cm.
Summary: During Haley's freshman year of high school, a campaign of
gossip and bullying causes her to be socially ostracized, but after
spending the summer living with her aunt, working at a resort, making
new friends, and dating a hunky lifeguard, she learns how to stand up
for herself and begins to trust again.
ISBN-13: 978-1-4169-3481-3 (hardcover)
ISBN-10: 1-4169-3481-2 (hardcover)
[1. Bullying—Fiction. 2. Self-esteem—Fiction. 3. Identity—Fiction.
4. Resorts—Fiction. 5. Aunts—Fiction. 6. High schools—Fiction.
7. Schools—Fiction.] I. Title.
PZ7.L9549De 2008
[Fic]—dc22
2007010945

FOR EVERY GIRL WHO HAS FOUND
THE COURAGE TO STAND UP
AND FIGHT BACK

Acknowledgments

• • •

I'm grateful to teens and adults everywhere who shared their stories with me, and to my fantastic readers, who asked for this book. As always, my sincere thanks to Emma Dryden, Lisa Cheng, and the entire team at McElderry Books.

Defying the Diva

Chapter One

I slid into my chair a nanosecond before the tardy bell and checked out the discussion-slash-quiz question scrawled on the chalkboard. Today's question was a two-parter. One: Discuss the following quote: "Blood sport is brought to its ultimate refinement in the gossip columns." Two: Identify the author.

I jotted down a couple of talking points in case Mrs. Westfall called on me, then considered the authorial options:

(A) Paris Hilton
(B) Christopher Isherwood
(C) Bernard Ingham
(D) Sylvester Stallone

Fortunately, Ingham's name had lodged in my brain when I skimmed the reading assignment the night before, so I was okay there. I flipped to a clean page as the lecture began, but I had trouble concentrating. For one thing I was worried about an overdue assignment for speech class that I just couldn't finish, mainly because most of the other kids were candidates for a starter colony of some alien race of superperformers, and I the complete and total introvert was severely intimidated. Plus, the year was winding down, and I was infected with a serious case of spring fever.

I gazed out the window. The relay team was running drills in the bright March sunshine, circling the cinder track in easy loops that were mesmerizing if you looked long enough. Beneath the flagpole a patch of yellow daffodils poked through the spring grass. The wide, Colorado sky was that perfect shade of blue that makes you impatient for summer.

"And so," Mrs. Westfall said, dragging me back to reality, "is Ingham's assertion a fair one? What about the writer of gossip?"

"Sometimes it gets bloody for them, too," Maddie Cooper offered from her chair in the back row. "Like that woman who writes all those unauthorized biographies of celebrities. I heard she got a lot of hate mail after her last book came out, and people accused her of making stuff up."

"Good point." Mrs. Westfall said, glancing at the clock on the wall. "To sum up, what is Ingham really saying here?"

"Never trust a journalist!" somebody said, and Mrs. Westfall laughed along with us.

I glanced at the stacks of newspapers, boxes of

clippings, tear sheets, and half-finished projects cluttering the table beneath the window. Even after nearly a whole year I sometimes had trouble believing my good luck. Due to a series of first-semester scheduling snafus so ridiculous that they'd make the Keystone Kops look like total geniuses, I had avoided the terminally boring freshman art-appreciation course I'd dreaded all last summer and wound up in Journalism One as the only freshman on the staff of the *Raider Review*. Mostly I was assigned to the routine stories the other staffers didn't want to bother with, until Maddie, a junior who wrote a supposedly anonymous gossip column called "In the Know," got sidelined with a raging case of mono and Mrs. Westfall appointed me to take her place.

Now Maddie was back, and my last column was set to run in Friday's edition. I scribbled in my notebook as Mrs. Westfall made a few final comments about responsibility in journalism and the fine line between innuendo and truth, blissfully unaware that by the end of the week the person who would know best about gossip and blood sport would be (E) Me. Haley Patterson.

A couple of days later I was halfway across the quad, heading for the humanities building, when Vanessa, one of my two best friends, called to me from the student parking lot. I shifted my backpack and waited for her to catch up. Dressed in her usual paint-spattered carpenter's overalls and faded T-shirt, she hurried across the sun-dappled quad, dodging clumps of fashionistas comparing shopping notes, jocks razzing each other about the upcoming basketball tournament, and math kids earnestly working out equations on their calculators. One of them, Sandi Ahrens, whom I'd known since we were seven years old and in Brownies together, looked up from her calculations and grinned at me, showing off her new, almost invisible braces.

"So what do you think, Haley? Way better than the old metal ones, huh?"

"Yeah."

Vanessa had stopped to talk to some guy from her pottery class, and I glanced at my watch, wishing she'd hurry.

"Not so geeky," Sandi went on. "I know I looked totally horrible before, but now maybe Harley will notice me. You think?" She glanced across the quad to where the object of her affection, a hulking ponytailed guy in baggy cargo pants and a sleeveless T-shirt that showed off his tattoos, was talking to a couple of other motorheads. "I bought this new shirt and everything."

Personally, I didn't understand the attraction, but why rain on her parade? "It could happen," I said. "You know how guys are."

Vanessa finished her conversation and jogged toward me.

"I have to go," I told Sandi. "I'm late for a meeting."

"Hey," Vanessa said, reaching me at last. "What's up?"

"An early meeting at the *Review* office. Supposedly Mrs. Westfall has some big announcement that can't wait till fifth period."

Vanessa shook her head. "I cannot believe how much

time you spend on that newspaper. You must be there at least twenty hours a week."

"Yeah, but it's the only good thing about high school since Jason dumped me."

"Hold it." Vanessa stopped me with one hand on my arm. "You aren't still upset about him are you?"

I shrugged. "He's a jerk."

"No argument there. And getting dumped totally sucks, but you are so much better off without him."

We reached the humanities building and went inside. I looked around for the third member of our group. "Where's Suzanne?"

"I have no idea, and don't change the subject."

"I have nothing else to say about Jason Finch except I wish he'd stop telling people I'm easy with every guy in school. It's disgusting."

"He's trying to make people think he's this big stud muffin so Carrie McMillan will go out with him. Nobody believes half the stuff he says."

"It's the half that they do pay attention to that I have to worry about."

"People who really know you know the truth, so quit worrying." We stopped in the hallway leading to the art studio, and Vanessa waggled her fingers at me. "See you at lunch."

I dumped some stuff in my locker and headed for the *Review* office. Vanessa was right; being on staff took up a huge chunk of time, but I didn't mind the long hours on flat nights when we got the paper ready for printing, or the pressures of keeping up with my classes while meeting deadlines. I loved knowing that on Friday every student in the school would be thumbing through the paper, reading my words.

I hurried into the *Review* office just as Mrs. Westfall announced a competition for an opinion column to be featured in next year's paper. Right away I started imagining the cool stuff I could write about if I won.

"There's not much time," she said, fingering the pearls at her throat. "You'll have one week to submit a five-hundred-word piece and synopses for four others." She perched on the corner of her gray metal desk and folded her arms. "I expect to see some mature, thoughtful pieces of journalism, people. No stories on proms, sports, or dating, okay?"

I scribbled "mature" and "thoughtful" in my notebook as she went on. "The writer whose work reflects the highest levels of quality and creativity will win the byline and will have a piece published in every issue of next year's *Review*."

Patrick Kelly, our editor in chief, winked at me, and I grinned back. Besides being a huge honor, having my own column would prove to my parents that I was just as talented as my brother Peyton, who had graduated with honors at midyear and was backpacking around the world before deciding among the top-college scholarships he'd been offered. A problem I never expect to have.

I looked around, sizing up the competition. As a senior Patrick would not be in the running. Maddie, the gossip column queen, was a shoo-in to replace Patrick next year, so she wouldn't bother with the competition either. The sports guy? Let's just say that if some sort of ball wasn't a major part of the story, he wasn't interested. That left Simone Hartwell, a quiet sophomore who came and went like a shadow, but whose work was always first-rate; Flip Morrison, who was the go-to guy for stories involving the school administration; and Emily French, Maddie's assistant, who was nicknamed Scoop because she liked to nose around and get the stories before anyone else.

Mrs. Westfall answered a few questions and reminded us of the deadline for the big double issue we were planning for the end of the year, and the meeting broke up just as the bell rang.

I skipped lunch and spent the whole day so preoccupied with ideas for my five stories that I didn't hear the final bell. I was still scribbling in my notebook when Mr. Richards, my history teacher, said, "Haley? You can go now." And I realized I was the only one left in the room.

I grabbed my backpack and looked out the window. Vanessa and Suzanne weren't yet at the flagpole, so I ran upstairs to my locker. As I headed back down, Patrick stopped me in the hallway.

"I assume you're going to enter the competition." He shifted his notebook to his other arm.

"Wild horses couldn't stop me."

"You've got a good chance. Mrs. Westfall really likes your work."

"Thanks. I just wish I had more experience writing

important stories. Most of my stuff is about the debate team and the new roof for the boys' gym. Like anyone cares."

Patrick grinned. "So it's not earth-shattering. You have to start somewhere."

"That's what Dad says."

"He should know."

Dad had been the editor of the *Ridgeview Record*, the only daily newspaper in town, since I was in second grade. Mom said he had ink in his veins instead of blood and that I was just the same.

"My internship at the *Record* was great," Patrick said as we started for the stairs. "Tell him I said thanks again for writing that college recommendation for me."

Just then Camilla Quinn, the queen bee of Ridgeview High, appeared with half a dozen of her loyal subjects and flashed a megawatt smile that did not include me. "Hi, Patrick."

"Hi."

"Listen, we're going over to the Burger Barn to grab a bite. Want to come?"

"No, thanks. I have to get home."

"Party pooper." She stuck her bottom lip out in an exaggerated pout. "That's what you always say."

"It's always true." Patrick let the seconds tick by until Camilla finally said, "Okay, then—be that way," and disappeared into the crush of students heading for the exits.

Patrick shook his head. "That's the third time this week. That girl just doesn't know when to give up."

"Obviously she has a huge crush on you," I said as we headed for the stairs.

"Not really," Patrick said. "It's a game she plays. Camilla wants only the things she can't get."

"She knows about Catherine?"

Patrick had been dating a girl from St. Thomas High School all year, and it was serious. One night when we were working late at the paper, Patrick told me that Catherine had totally been there for him when his dad died, and that he could not imagine his future without her in it.

Now he said, "I'm sure Camilla knows about Catherine, but it doesn't make any difference. Camilla thinks she should decide who's in and who's out and that everybody else exists just to carry out her wishes. I'm not buying into it."

As we reached the second-floor landing, Patrick turned toward the *Review* office. "Gotta grab my stuff and then I'm out of here."

I waved to him and went outside. Suzanne and Vanessa were sitting by the flagpole, books open on their laps.

"Haley!" Suzanne snapped her copy of *Jane Eyre* shut and tucked a strand of honey-gold hair behind her ear. "What *took* you so long? And where were you at lunch? We were about to send out a search party."

"Sorry." I dropped onto the soft spring grass beside Suzanne. "I should have told you. I skipped lunch to work on a thing for the paper, plus I had to turn in an overdue assignment for speech class."

"You're lucky Ms. Costello let you turn it in late," Suzanne said. "Last semester, when Coach Roberts taught that class, he wouldn't let us get away with anything."

"At least he didn't make you memorize Shakespeare."

"No kidding! What a nightmare!" Just then some guy yelled her name. Suzanne looked up and waved to him.

Vanessa grinned. "We lucked out. How are old Romeo and Juliet coming along?"

I fished my sunglasses out of my backpack. "It's going okay. We're doing the key scenes from each act instead of the whole play. At least Ms. Costello double-cast everything, so I have to go onstage only once."

Suzanne nodded. "I heard that you and Camilla were taking turns narrating."

"We flipped a coin. She's going first."

"Why doesn't that surprise me?" Vanessa folded a stick of gum into her mouth. "I heard that Sabrina and Ryan are totally into playing the poor doomed lovers. I heard they're putting in a lot of extra practice. If you get my drift."

"Hey, you should put that in your gossip column," Suzanne said. "It's way more exciting than who's going to be elected Most Likely to Succeed."

"Shut up!" I swatted Suzanne's arm, and she grinned. "The column is supposed to be anonymous."

"Oh, right," Suzanne said. "There must be at least one person on the planet who hasn't figured out you're the one who has been subbing for Maddie."

"I don't care. Maddie's back, and my last one comes out tomorrow."

"What a relief!" Suzanne teased. "Now maybe we'll get some actual gossip instead of more speculation about who will win Class Favorites this year." She rolled her eyes. "Borrring!"

"What did you expect? I'm not exactly a regular on the A-list party circuit. It's hard to write stuff that's interesting without being mean."

"Maddie doesn't pull many punches," Vanessa said. "Remember when she hinted that Becca Rosenberg was bulimic? And it turned out to be true? And that item about those two football players who had their licenses suspended for drunk driving?"

"Maddie calls it as she sees it," Suzanne said. "She loves stuff about people's personal lives. She knows what everybody wants to read about."

"Yeah, but I'm just not into gossip as a blood sport."

"Whatever." Vanessa popped her gum and shaded her eyes with one hand. "How did your emergency meeting at the paper go?"

"Mrs. Westfall is running a competition to pick a columnist for next year. I'm dying to win."

"You will," Suzanne said. "I know you will."

"Thanks. I've got a million ideas. The hard part is choosing one. I'm supposed to write about something important."

Vanessa let her geometry book slide to the ground and folded her arms across her chest. "Who's going to judge this so-called competition?"

"Careful," Suzanne said. "Your cynicism is showing."

"Mrs. Westfall, I guess."

"In other words," Vanessa said, narrowing her eyes, "it's rigged."

"She'll be fair," I said.

Vanessa snorted. "I wouldn't count on it."

Suzanne and I exchanged a grin. Last year's study of American politics, coupled with an addiction to the talk shows on CNN, had made Vanessa distrustful of authority figures. Trying to change her mind was an exercise in futility, so I said, "I'm starved. Let's eat."

"I'm game." Suzanne stood and pulled Vanessa to her feet. "Come on, sunshine, let's go."

We left campus and walked up three blocks to the Burger Barn. The food was only so-so, but it was budget-friendly, and the guy who ran the place was pretty tolerant. Unless somebody got really loud, or seemed about to actually throw a punch, Ralph stayed in back flipping burgers and making fries, letting us stay at the tables as long as we wanted.

Suzanne scored a table by the window, and after we ordered fries and Cokes, she launched into a detailed description of her latest shopping trip with her sister, who was majoring in fashion design at the university where my mom taught English Lit. Fiona dressed Suzanne like a model in a fashion magazine, pairing distressed jeans with a sparkly top and an alligator belt, or suede boots with a short skirt and tights. After we admired Suzanne's latest acquisition, a beaded lariat necklace, Vanessa rhapsodized about the Ratt Finks, her favorite band of the month, and I tried out a couple of story ideas for the competition.

"All you think about is that paper," Vanessa complained. "You need to broaden your horizons, girlfriend."

"Oh, like *you're* so well-rounded."

Vanessa obsessed about art and music the way I did about writing. She walked around with paint under her fingernails and bits of clay in her hair from some pot-throwing adventure, and she listened to her MP3 player until it had practically attached itself to her skin like an extra body part.

"Here you go, ladies." Ralph delivered our order and went back to his grill. Suzanne pointed a fry at me. "When summer gets here, you'll have to find some other way to occupy your time."

"I'll be at my aunt's while my parents are overseas." I salted my fries and popped one into my mouth. "Exiled in Copper Springs."

"Mom and I went to the spa there last year," Vanessa said. "When she was trying to recover from the divorce. It's not so bad."

"Maybe not for one day, but for the entire summer?" I toyed with the ketchup bottle. "I won't know anybody except for my aunt, and I'll miss out on everything here."

"Vanessa and I could come up there for a week," Suzanne said. "They have a pool, right?"

"I can't," Vanessa said. "I have two months of court-ordered visitation with my dad, and he enrolled me in some totally lame science camp in New Jersey. Some visitation."

"Then I'll come," Suzanne said, patting my arm. "Don't worry, Haley baby. We won't let you fall off the face of the earth."

"And when we all get back here in September, we'll have a major catching-up party," Vanessa said. "We'll blow a whole weekend. It'll be fun."

The door opened, and Camilla and company breezed in. Superdiva sauntered over to the order window and leaned in to speak to Ralph, who hung on her every word like he was sixteen instead of sixty. He came out from behind the counter, cleaned off the best table in the house, which had just been vacated by a horde of football players, and seated Camilla with a flourish. The other girls in her entourage crowded around her, laughing, vying for her attention.

"Man," Suzanne said softly, "look at her. Everybody bends over backward for her, like she's a queen or something."

"She's a phony," Vanessa muttered, dragging a fry through the pool of ranch dressing on the side of her plate. "She's all lovey-dovey when she wants something from you, but once she gets it, watch out. I don't trust her even a little bit."

"I still wouldn't mind being friends with her," Suzanne said. "Nobody messes with you when you're in her circle. And I heard the party she threw last weekend was awesome. All the most popular boys were there."

"Of course they were," Vanessa said. "How many boys could resist the chance to party with the famous Jack Quinn?"

I didn't pay much attention to the athletic scene, but around Ridgeview you'd have to be dead not to know about Camilla's dad, a home-grown football hero who had broken every high-school record on the books before going on to college and a brilliant career in the NFL. Then one night an eighteen-wheeler hit Jack's SUV on the interstate. Now he owned Bronco Motors, the town's biggest auto dealership, and presided at Camilla's endless parties, where he tossed footballs from his wheelchair and ran films of his old games in the home theater in the basement. He and our principal, Mr. Parsons, had been teammates back in high school. Mr. Quinn occasionally stopped in at school to check on the ad he regularly placed in the *Review* and to reminisce with Mr. Parsons about their glory days.

"Omigod." Suzanne set down her glass with such force that her soda slopped onto the table. "She's coming this way."

"Hang on, I'll alert CNN," Vanessa said as Camilla and her friends wove through the crowded restaurant and stopped at our table.

Camilla tossed her hair and smiled down at us. "Hey, girls, what's going on?"

Suzanne, suddenly ultracasual, said, "Nothing much, just chilling. Waiting for summer vacation. You know."

"Yeah," Camilla said. "School is really beginning to get on my nerves. Luckily, my gran is coming to the rescue." She paused to be sure we were all paying proper attention. "She's taking me to New York in a couple of weeks, and I absolutely cannot wait! We're going to hit the stores and go sightseeing. And Gran is getting tickets for that hot musical. The one about the witches."

"Relatives of yours?" Vanessa murmured.

Camilla ignored her. "Haley. What's up at the old paper? Heard any good gossip lately?"

"That's not really my department."

"Oh, right," Camilla said. "I forgot. You're a *serious* journalist. Why, I wouldn't be surprised if you win the Howitzer Prize someday."

The girls in her entourage laughed.

"It's the *Pulitzer* Prize, you moron," Vanessa muttered, stuffing another fry into her mouth.

"Excuse me?" Camilla said. "Did I miss something?"

Suzanne said, "Vanessa's in a bad mood. Don't pay any attention to her."

"I never do." Camilla turned back to me. "Anyhow, Haley, I was wondering if you'd like to come to my St. Patrick's Day party this weekend."

Suzanne actually gasped. Vanessa stopped chewing. I stared at Camilla like she'd sprouted an extra head.

Camilla went on. "I've decided it's time to widen my circle, and I've never invited anybody from the paper. I thought it might be fun if you and Patrick came. He could dress up as his namesake. Maybe even dye his hair green. Wouldn't that be fun?"

"Yeah," Vanessa said. "A barrel of laughs."

Camilla gave me credit for having a lot more influence over Patrick than I really did, but even if I'd wanted to go to her party, the contest at the paper was way more important.

"I can't," I said. "But maybe Patrick would like to go. You could ask him."

Suzanne kicked me under the table.

One of Camilla's loyal subjects, a freckle-faced girl who played first violin in the school orchestra, said, "She already did, but he said no."

Camilla whirled around. "Shut up, Gracie."

She spun back around and said, "Let me get this straight. You're turning down my invitation, just like that?"

"I don't have time." I ate a couple of fries. "Big project at the paper, and I have less than a week to get it done."

Gracie and the rest of them looked shell-shocked.

"Fine," Camilla said. "Forget I ever asked." Hands on her hips, she turned to my friends. "Suzanne? Would you like to come?"

Suzanne's mouth worked, but for a moment nothing came out. Finally she said, "You mean it?"

"Sure. Why not. You too, Vanessa."

Before either of them could say anything more, She Who Must Be Obeyed said, "Eight o'clock. Saturday. My house."

She motioned to her friends, and they left the Burger Barn, arms linked, heads thrown back, as if Planet Earth had been invented just for them.

I stood up. "I have to go. Are you coming?"

"I think I'll hang out here a little longer," Suzanne said, her voice high and strange.

Vanessa said, "Then I have to stay too. She's giving me a ride home."

I walked home, feeling let down and left out. I didn't care about missing Camilla's party—most of the girls in her crowd were emaciated blondes with major shopping addictions—but I minded a lot that Suzanne seemed more interested in Camilla than in me. I hoped that once Suzanne saw how phony Camilla and her crowd were, she'd come to her senses and everything would get back to normal.

The next morning, when Dad dropped me at school, Mr. Quinn's van was parked in the drive, and Mr. Parsons was talking to Mr. Quinn though the open driver's-side window. As I came up the walk, Mr. Parsons held up the new edition of the *Review* and gave me a thumbs-up. My story about a Ridgeview grad who had won an important science prize at MIT was a last-minute addition to page five, and Mrs. Westfall had given me a rare byline—icing on the cake. "Good job, Miss Patterson."

"Thanks!"

I went inside, pretty much walking on air, until Suzanne grabbed my arm and shoved her copy of the paper in my face, bringing me back to earth.

"Traitor!"

"What are you talking about?"

People swirled around us, chattering and laughing. It was Friday, the basketball team was playing a tournament game that night, and everyone was keyed up, looking forward to the pep rally and the caravan to the game in Taylorsville.

"What am I talking about? This!" As the crowd ebbed and flowed around us, Suzanne pointed to an item in the "In The Know" column. "'What cute freshman girl is totally gaga about which junior basketball player? Hint: They share the same initials, SD.' How *could* you, Haley?"

It had taken only one dance during homecoming for Suzanne to develop a full-blown crush on Sean Davis. For weeks afterward she flirted with him in the cafeteria, left notes for him in his homeroom desk, "accidentally" ran into him in the library, and went out of her way to walk past his locker between classes. All of which Sean religiously ignored.

Now I said, "I'm sorry! I was really desperate for material, and it's not like your crush on Sean was a huge secret. But I didn't mean to get you all upset."

"Who wouldn't be upset?" Suzanne said. "Having their love life exposed in front of the whole school."

"Just yesterday you said you wanted juicy stuff! You said I should write about Sabrina and Ryan, remember?"

"That's different."

"So it's okay to dish about other people, just not you?" Suzanne rolled her eyes.

"Nobody pays that much attention to this stupid column anyway."

"At least you could have warned me, instead of springing it on me out of the blue."

"You're right. I should have. I was worried about finishing my homework, and I wasn't thinking. Come on, Suze, give me a break. I won't write about you ever again. I promise."

The first bell rang. Suzanne stuffed the paper into her math book as we headed for our lockers. "You are impossible. I don't know why I'm friends with you."

"Because I let you borrow all my best stuff," I said. "Because I cover for you when you break curfew, because—"

"Forget it, dumbass." One corner of her mouth lifted in a little half smile. "Only, in the future, keep my private stuff private, okay?"

We got to the top of the stairs, and there stood Suzanne's green-eyed, messy-haired basketball hero, with a couple of his teammates.

"Haley," Sean said. "Interesting item in the paper today. I wonder who this 'SD' could be."

They laughed and headed down the hall. Suzanne shot me a murderous look.

Just then Camilla shoved her way through the crowd, slamming locker doors shut on her way toward me. "There you are, you little bitch."

I grabbed my lit book and my favorite reporter's notebook, the one with Monet's lilies on the cover. "Excuse me, I'll be late for class."

The bell rang and people scattered, but Camilla stood there, blocking my way. Suzanne dawdled at her locker, pretending to look for something.

Camilla waved her copy of the *Review* under my nose and said, "Being late for class is the least of your problems, Patterson. Who gave you permission to write about my party?"

"Haven't you heard? Here in the good old U.S. of A. there is a thing called freedom of the press. You'd know that if you ever paid attention to anything except your manicure."

"'Partygoers say the scene at Camilla Quinn's bash last Saturday night was wilder than usual,'" Camilla read. "'With plenty of food, drink, and music, and no parents on the premises, revelers partied until well past the two a.m. city curfew.'" She ripped the page in half and wadded it into a tight little ball. "You weren't even there! How would you know what happened?"

Suzanne slammed her locker shut. "Everybody was talking about that party, Camilla. It would have been hard for Haley not to have heard about it."

I sent Suzanne a grateful look and made a mental note to buy her a really stupendous birthday present. A designer bag, maybe. Or a convertible.

Camilla's mouth dropped open. "You're sticking up for her? After she humiliated you with that crack about you and Sean Davis? Don't you know the whole school pities you, the poor little freshman nobody, pining after a guy who barely knows she's alive?"

Suzanne looked stricken. "Really?"

"Yes, really. I can't believe you still want to be friends with her." Camilla wheeled back to me. "You made a huge mistake, Haley. Thanks to your big mouth Dad just called me into the principal's office and canceled my trip to New York. And you will be very, very sorry."

I tried not to let Camilla's threat bother me. During a boring lecture in PE, I fooled around with some ideas for the competition at the paper and caught up on my reading for Freshman Lit. That afternoon at the pep rally I sat with Suzanne and Vanessa, and we stomped and clapped and tried to out-cheer the upperclassmen. On Saturday we hit the mall, shopping for the stuff Vanessa needed for her upcoming camping adventure in New Jersey. We stopped at the food court for Cokes and fries and ate at a table decorated with a bunch of glittery green shamrocks. All Suzanne could talk about was what to wear to the party at Camilla's that night and whether any hot guys would show up.

"I thought she was grounded." I sipped my soda and watched a bunch of green balloons drift toward the ceiling.

"Her trip to New York is off," Suzanne said, "but her dad caved about the party. She invited so many people it would have been too hard to cancel at the last minute." She ate a couple of fries. "You shouldn't have turned her down, Haley. This is going to be the best party of our lives."

Vanessa rolled her eyes. "Don't worry, Haley, we'll fill you in later."

"Like I care." My whole world had suddenly gone haywire. Anger flared inside my chest. "I have to go."

A few nights later Patrick and I were working late at

the paper, finishing stories for the last regular issues and for the graduation edition planned for the end of May. Everyone else had already left. In the hallway the night custodians were moving around, emptying trash cans and vacuuming the carpets in the senior lounge. While I waited for our ancient printer to spit out the last of my captions, I filed a stack of papers and neatened up my workspace, taking in the familiar smells of paper and ink, and the slightly sulfuric stench of some long-ago science experiment.

"Ready to call it a night?" Patrick stuck his head over the top of his cubicle.

"All finished." I checked the page I'd laid out that afternoon. It looked great, with just the right mix of copy, graphics, and white space. I grabbed my jacket and switched off my computer.

Outside, the bus returning the basketball team from their last tournament game pulled into the parking lot. Patrick waved to the security guard, and we went out to the parking lot, where the team and the cheerleaders were piling into cars, heading for the after-game parties. Camilla was standing on the front lawn, drinking a soda and talking with a couple of other cheerleaders.

"You need a ride home?" Patrick asked.

"Mom is picking me up. She's at some departmental thing at the university. It's supposed to be over by ten thirty."

The bus pulled out of the drive in a cloud of fumes. The parking lot emptied. "I wish she'd hurry."

"Here." Patrick took off his letter jacket and draped it over my shoulders. "We can sit on that bench by the pond, out of the wind."

"You don't have to wait with me," I said. "I'll be okay."

"It's no problem," Patrick said. "With seven sisters around, my house is so chaotic. I could use a few minutes of total quiet."

We walked to the pond. I dropped my book bag on the ground and settled onto the bench, tucking Patrick's jacket around me.

Patrick stretched out his skinny legs and rubbed his temples. "I'm beat."

I was bone tired too, but it was the good kind of fatigue, that feeling you get when you know you've accomplished something important.

"What about your article for the competition?" Patrick asked. "All finished?"

"Almost. It's about the pressure in high school to be an overachiever and whether it makes any difference in real life."

"It guarantees that you'll go through high school feeling sleep-deprived, but overachievers get into the best colleges," Patrick said. "I'm lucky I didn't even want to go Ivy League. I don't have the grades or the money." He shrugged. "I don't know. Maybe I'll be sorry someday when some Yale grad gets the job I really want."

"But that's just it! People make themselves sick trying to get perfect SATs, competing for the highest class rank and a National Merit, and for what? If you look at the guys who are running the biggest companies in the whole country—and most of them *are* guys—hardly any of them went to the big name schools. Some of the richest ones never even graduated college at all."

"Whoa," Patrick said. "You *have* been working hard."

"Practically the whole weekend. I'm fairly sleep-deprived myself."

He grinned. "No partying at Camilla's on Saturday night?"

"Nope. Suzanne and Vanessa went. It's all Suzanne has talked about this week."

"I can believe Suzanne would buy into Camilla's games," Patrick said, "but I thought Vanessa had more backbone than that."

"She talks tough, but she's just like the rest of us, wanting to fit in."

"She'd have an easier time of it if she didn't dress so weird," Patrick said. "That girl is scary."

A police cruiser drove past. A freight train rumbled through the other side of town. I glanced at my watch, wishing Mom would hurry. I had tons of math homework due the next day, and an overdue project for science class.

Then a voice behind us said, "Oh. My. God."

Camilla stepped out of the shadows. Her red and white spangled top glittered in the light from the street lamp; her short white skirt swirled around her legs. She peered at us and said, "God, Patrick, what are you doing hanging around with a loser like Haley? Haven't you heard about her reputation?"

"What are you talking about, Camilla?" Patrick said.

"She's wearing your *jacket*?" Camilla went on, laughing. "Oh, this is *really* rich! Patrick Kelly, the editor of the paper, hasn't heard the big news. Well, here's the headline, Patrick: Your little mascot is nothing but a slut. Jason says she'll do it with anybody. That's why he dumped her."

Anger boiled up inside me, hot as road tar in August. "Jason is a liar."

Camilla ignored me. "Her new name is Haley the Ho. I'd get a clue if I were you, Patrick. It would be too bad if Catherine found out you were hanging around after hours with somebody like her."

Five minutes before, Patrick had been acting like his normal, sweet, sensible self. Now, despite his earlier comment about Camilla, I could actually feel him pulling back and a huge empty space opening up between us. A chill that had nothing to do with the sharp night wind ran down my spine. He stood.

"It's getting late. Guess I'll head home."

I handed him his jacket just as a horn sounded and Mom pulled into the drive. I grabbed my book bag and pushed past Camilla. Her laugh followed me across the parking lot. Mom chattered the whole way home about the faculty party and the article she'd just had accepted for publication, but I was only half listening.

When we pulled into our driveway, she switched off the engine. "Are you okay? You're so quiet tonight."

"I'm fine." I got out of the car and hurried inside. Mom came in behind me.

"Haley? Can't we at least talk for a minute?" She set her purse and keys on the table in the entry hall. "How about some milk and a piece of pie? There's some left from dinner."

"God, no, Mom! I'm already huge."

"You are not huge. You're just fine for your height, and a piece of pie every once in a while never hurt anybody."

"I'm not hungry. And I've got tons of homework."

"You're spending too much time at that paper. It's wearing you down."

I escaped to my room, pulled out my cell, and hit speed dial.

"Hey," Suzanne said.

Music was playing in the background. I pictured Suzanne in her poster-filled room, her books and papers scattered everywhere and her CDs blasting away.

"It's me," I said, my voice tight with anger. "You'll never guess what happened tonight."

I told her everything that had just happened. Suzanne didn't say a word.

"What's the matter with you?" I yelled. "She's trying to get even with me because of that *stupid* gossip column, which was so *not* my idea in the first place!"

"Maybe you should have thought of that before," Suzanne said. "Camilla is really upset about disappointing her grandmother and missing her big trip."

"Whose side are you on, anyway?"

"Look, Haley," Suzanne said, "this is not a good time. I have to go."

Then a familiar laugh came over the phone. *Camilla.*

"Suzanne? Wait!"

Click.

Chapter Two

By third period the next day the Campaign to Destroy Haley was in full swing. Nobody, not even Vanessa, would talk to me. Girls I had known since elementary school crossed to the other side of the hallway and turned their backs as I walked from my locker to class, as if we were back in third grade, avoiding cooties.

I yanked open the classroom door and slid into my seat, ignoring the veiled looks and the whispers swirling around me. I opened my book, but the words swam on the page, as incomprehensible as Swahili.

Just as Mr. Aljancic came in, a piece of notebook paper folded into a tight little square landed on my desk and sat there like a bomb waiting to explode. I could feel everyone watching, waiting for me to read it. I pretended not to see it, even after Mr. Aljancic noticed it and frowned at me like I'd just drowned a litter of kittens.

The tardy bell rang, and Mr. Aljancic started lecturing about the main characters in *Lord of the Flies* and how each of them experienced a defining moment—that one fragment of time when a decision is made that changes the person forever. I tried to pay attention—Lit was one class I normally enjoyed—but right then all I could think about was Camilla's plan to wreck my life. I couldn't believe that Suzanne was willing to sacrifice our friendship for admission to Camilla's world, even though I sort of understood it. Suzanne's dad was a Marine pilot who uprooted the family every few years whenever his assignment changed, and Suzanne was the perpetual new kid, desperate to belong.

Vanessa was more of a mystery. She'd never made a secret of her scorn for people like Camilla, who used others to get what they wanted. But that hadn't stopped her from turning her back on me too. Hot tears scalded my eyes and blurred the pages of my book.

Mr. Aljancic dropped one hand onto my shoulder, and then I remembered where I was. Third-period lit class. Savages. Choices. Defining moments. He scooped up the paper bomb lying on my desk and said, "Am I boring you, Haley?"

"No, sir."

"Then suppose you read the passage we were just discussing."

He saw that I was totally lost and that he had made his point. "Page one thirty-six," he said tiredly, slipping my unread note into his pocket. "Please try to pay attention."

Every day from then on Camilla and her minions devised some new form of torture. Nasty notes addressed to Haley the Ho appeared in my locker. In PE, even though I was a decent athlete, I was the last to be chosen for teams. I sat alone at the far end of the bleachers watching as the daily team captains chose up sides for basketball drills.

One morning Sabrina Brooks, aka Juliet in our upcoming spring production, was chosen as one of the captains, and I had a moment of hope. Sabrina and I had been practicing lines together during rehearsals, ignoring the smirks Camilla sent our way every time Ms. Costello's back was turned. I thought maybe Sabrina might pick me before I was left dead last on the bleachers again. Carrie McMillan, my ex-boyfriend Jason's new squeeze, was the other captain, so I knew there was no help coming from her. Carrie tossed her perfect mahogany-brown ponytail and scanned the class.

"Amy," Carrie said, getting first dibs on the best athlete in the class.

Then it was Sabrina's turn. I stared hard at her, willing her to choose me, just once. But Sabrina looked right past me and picked Beth Whitehead, a popular girl with the dribbling and shooting skills of an amoeba. Beth jumped up and trotted over to Sabrina's side of the gym, her sneakers squeaking on the polished wood.

Sabrina whispered something to Carrie, who nodded and looked right at me before choosing another girl. And that was how it went, back and forth between the two captains until only Sandi Ahrens and I were left.

Hot, salty tears started behind my eyes as Coach Miller blew her whistle and said, "Okay, Sandi, you're with Carrie. Haley, you're on Sabrina's team. Let's go!"

I could feel Sandi's eyes on me. I stared up at the bright gym lights as the game began, mentally counting down the days until summer vacation.

\\\\//

April Fool's Day arrived. Traditionally it was a big deal at Ridgeview: People wore their shirts backward, sent each other fake text messages, switched the signs on the restroom doors, and just generally acted crazy. Occasionally a few of the teachers got into the act, announcing a major quiz when there really wasn't one, or putting out-of-order signs on the soda machines. This year the big day fell on Sunday, but the following day the whole junior class showed up wearing black, and a couple of chemistry geniuses set off the fire alarm during third period. For me it got personal. Somebody poured a whole tube of Krazy Glue into my backpack, ruining my homework and three library books. As soon as I sat down for lunch, every girl at the table got up and moved.

I threw my lunch away and went out to the quad. I sat on the ground in the corner and made myself as small as possible. Closing my eyes, I let the sunshine warm my face, wondering how I could ever survive the rest of freshman year.

"Haley."

Patrick squatted beside me and dropped his books onto the grass. "Why are you sitting here by yourself?"

"You know why. I'm the pariah of this whole school. Not that you care."

"Not everyone hates you."

"Oh, really? You could have fooled me. Even Mrs. Westfall has stopped talking to me, except when she absolutely has to."

"She's not talking much to Emily or Simone or Flip, either," Patrick said. "She's judging the writing competition, and she doesn't want any of you to think she's playing favorites."

"I'm not anybody's favorite."

"Look," Patrick said. "I'm sorry if it seems like I'm avoiding you. I couldn't care less what Camilla thinks, but you know how crazy I am about Catherine, and her family is really strict. If she found out about—"

I got to my feet and pushed past him. "You don't have to spell it out. I get it."

I left him there in the quad and slogged through the rest of my day, feeling like I was trapped in one of those glass booths they put beauty contestants in to keep them from hearing the other contestants' answers to last-round questions. People were talking, laughing, slamming lockers, hurrying to beat the tardy bell, popping open soda cans, sending and receiving text messages. I could see it all, yet I felt completely isolated from everything going on around me.

That night after I finished my homework, I was surfing

the net, trying to keep my mind off school and the fact that there were still two months of torture to go, when the letter box icon popped up. *You've got mail.*

I should have had more sense than to open it without even checking to see who sent it but the subject line, *Save the date!!* seemed like an invitation, and I was so desperate I didn't care if it was nothing more than an announcement of an upcoming shoe sale at Happy Feet. I clicked it open.

Haley the Ho,

We have taken a vote and decided that next Monday is the day you should kill yourself. Face it, you're the biggest loser at Ridgeview High, and your life is over anyway. Do us all a favor so we don't have to keep looking at your gigantic hippo butt and your ugly face.

The sender's name jumped out at me then as if it had been written in hot pink neon. *QuinntessentialGrl.* Camilla. My stomach heaved. I barely made it to the bathroom before I threw up. I sat on the cold tile floor, sour bile burning my throat, and thought about how peaceful it would be not to have to face Camilla and the rest of them ever again. A picture of Peyton's friend Joe Bob Turner flashed through my head, as stark as if I were seeing him in a strobe light. I was barely thirteen when he died in the field house at school in what his parents insisted was a horrible accident, even after they found his note explaining everything.

Like Peyton, Joe Bob was a success at everything he tried. I couldn't believe he'd take his own life, but now I understood the utter despair and howling aloneness that had driven him to the edge where there was no turning back. I wondered how he'd gotten up the nerve to do what he did, what he'd felt in his last moments. I wondered if I could be that brave. I wondered if it would hurt.

"Haley?" Mom came in and bent down to brush my damp hair off my face, pulling me back from my dark thoughts. "What's the matter, honey?"

Mom was the type of parent who thought she could fix whatever went wrong in my life. If I told her what was happening, especially if I told her about the e-mail, she'd go straight to the principal. Then Camilla and the rest of them would make my life ten times worse.

"Must have been the cafeteria food." I got to my feet. "I feel better now, Mom."

"Are you sure?" She felt my forehead, checking for fever the way she used to when I was five and prone to ear infections. "Maybe you should take something to settle your stomach."

I brushed my teeth and splashed cool water on my face. "I'm okay. Just need some sleep."

"You're working too hard at that paper," Mom said. "You're just like your father. You never know when enough is enough."

I went back to my room, trashed the evil e-mail, and crawled into bed, exhausted.

The next morning I stood in the shower until my hands

shriveled, trying to get up the nerve to face another day. I couldn't remember the last time I'd eaten. My clothes were getting loose. I burrowed inside them, too miserable to pay attention in class, and the teachers didn't even notice.

I dressed and went downstairs just as Dad was leaving for the paper. Mom had already left for a faculty meeting at the university; her breakfast plate and coffee mug were in the sink.

"Morning, sweetheart." Dad planted a kiss on my head. "How are things at *your* paper?"

"Great, Dad. The last regular issue comes out a week from Friday."

"Don't forget to save me a copy." He picked up his coffee mug and his briefcase and headed for the door. "Can you catch the bus this morning? I'd drop you at school, but I'm swamped at the office. Need to get in early before the interruptions start."

"Sure. No problem." I poured a cup of coffee and opened a package of sweetener.

He turned back to me, his red tie slightly askew, his hand resting on the doorknob. "Are you okay, Haley? You seem distracted. And you hardly eat anything at all." He waved one hand at me. "You should be having milk and juice, some cereal. Something besides coffee."

Too wrung out to argue, I fixed a bowl of Wheat-O's and choked down a few bites while he watched.

Satisfied, my father punched the button to raise the garage door. "See you tonight. Maybe we'll take in a movie."

"Okay." I rinsed my cereal bowl, finished getting ready

for the torture chamber, and headed for the bus stop.

The bus was about half full. I sat alone at the back, watching normal people starting their day: a knot of young mothers in exercise gear waiting at the corner with their baby strollers and Starbucks cups, a few guys from the Ridgeview High track team jogging through Centennial Park, two girls in a dusty black Jeep bobbing their heads to loud music as they waited for the traffic light to change.

At Sixth Avenue and Gardiner, the bus ground to a halt, and Sandi Ahrens climbed on. Without waiting for an invitation she made her way to the back of the bus and plopped down beside me. "Hi, Haley."

"Hi." I watched the Jeep speed past the bus and slip through the early morning traffic. Sandi put one hand on my shoulder and said softly, "It sucks, huh?"

"I'm okay."

"Right. And I'm Cleopatra." She dug through her backpack, came up with two sticks of gum and offered me one. When I shook my head, she unwrapped a piece and popped it into her mouth. "Look, Haley. People like us? We have to stick together, you know?"

"I'm not like you! God! Just leave me alone, okay?"

Tears sprang to her eyes. "Forget it."

She hoisted her backpack and lurched up the aisle to an empty seat. I felt like a shallow jerk, but I just couldn't dig myself into an even deeper hole by hanging out with her.

The bus chugged to a stop, and I headed inside. A couple of boys I didn't know were standing at my locker elbowing each other and laughing. I shoved them aside and froze in horror. The door was plastered with dozens of little foil squares.

"Haley Ho," one of the boys said, "can I give you my phone number? Maybe we can hook up later."

"Shut up." I started ripping the condom packets off the door, hiding them in my backpack before anyone else could see.

The other guy snickered. "Oh, look, she's saving them for later. Maybe you've got a chance, Ricky."

Vanessa and Suzanne were standing beside the water cooler with a couple of other girls, watching the whole show. I pushed past the boys and went over to my former friends, tears running down my face. "Why are you just standing there? Why don't you *do* something?" I cried.

"As if you don't know," Suzanne said.

"I *said* I was sorry about that stupid gossip column. It wasn't that bad."

The first bell rang, and people scattered. Camilla and her top lieutenants rounded the corner and stopped short. "Suzanne!" Camilla barked.

And like one of those trained seals at Sea World, Suzanne whirled around and sprinted down the hall toward Camilla. There she turned her back to me as the girls formed a huddle and whispered together, their arms wound tightly around each other's waists.

"Vanessa." I hated admitting how close I was to a complete meltdown, but I couldn't help it. "You have to help me."

Her expression softened, and for a split second I felt a

glimmer of hope. A locker clanged shut. Camilla's laughter drifted down the hallway. Vanessa glanced at the knot of girls standing outside the chemistry lab.

"I hate what she's doing to you," Vanessa muttered. "It's totally unfair."

"Then *do* something! Talk some sense into Suzanne."

"She won't listen. It's like Camilla has put her under some kind of weird spell. I can't stop anything. And if I defend you, Camilla will turn on me, too."

"You've never cared what Camilla thought!"

"Yeah, but I don't want the whole school making fun of me."

Just then Camilla called, "Vanessa? Are you coming?"

"I gotta go." Vanessa hitched her battered leather backpack onto her shoulder.

"Coward! I hate you!"

Vanessa walked away without looking back.

Chapter Three

Monday. Death Day. I skipped school, figuring no one would miss me. Mom was buried under a mountain of final exam papers and the million details of her upcoming trip to England. Dad had left the day before for Cleveland, where he was giving a speech to a group of newspaper editors.

Alone in the house, I turned the phones off, locked the doors, and crawled under the covers, the hateful e-mail playing over and over in my head. *Loser. Your life is over . . . do us a favor . . .*

A warm spring rain pattered at the windows. Tires hissed on the wet pavement. I heard the bus arrive at my stop on the corner, and the grinding of gears as it pulled away. I punched my pillow and pulled the covers over my head, hoping that once Camilla realized I was absent, the high-school rumor mill would kick into warp speed, the whispers and what-ifs would start, and she'd worry that I *had* killed myself and she would be blamed. Maybe Vanessa would get scared enough to talk, and the adults would get a clue without my having to be the one who blew the whistle.

But just after eleven o'clock I heard Mom's car pull into the garage. A couple of minutes later her footsteps pounded up the stairs, and she burst into my room without bothering to knock. "Haley?"

"Hi, Mom." I blinked and stretched, pretending I'd been asleep.

"Haley, the school called, wondering where you were. Then I called here and you didn't pick up. You scared me half to death!"

"I'm sorry. I overslept."

Mom kicked off her shoes and sat cross-legged on my bed. "Look, sweetie, I know Daddy and I have been preoccupied lately, tying up loose ends at work and getting ready for our trip, but if something's wrong, if you're in some kind of trouble, you can tell me. You know that."

"I'm okay."

"No." Mom shook her head. "You are *not* okay. You hide out in your room all the time. It's been weeks since I've seen any of your friends over here. And just look at you. You've lost weight, and you never bother with your hair or your clothes anymore." She sighed. "All those cute spring outfits you bought with your Christmas money are hanging in the closet gathering dust."

"Vanessa and Suzanne are mad at me. But I can handle it. Besides, school's almost over, and then you and Dad will be on your way to London and I'll be up at Aunt Bitsy's."

The expression on Mom's face said it all: She couldn't wait to start her lectures in England. Dad had a ton of unused vacation time saved up and was going with her. Peyton had offered to come home for the summer to keep an eye on me, but thanks to his underdeveloped supervisory skills, I was headed for an entire summer in lovely Copper Springs. Even though the plan had been in place for months, I felt lost. Abandoned.

Now Mom's brain slid into a whole other gear. She started to pace. "Remind me to call Bitsy tonight. And we need to get you some new shorts and a sweater. It can get cool up in the mountains at night. I should make another list. But right now I need to call the school and tell them you're coming in late."

"There's an assembly this afternoon," I lied. "And I have journalism lab fifth period. I won't miss any classes. Please, Mom, let me stay home."

"You see what I mean?" Mom said. "Skipping school. This is not like you, Haley." She sucked in a quick breath as if a new thought had suddenly occurred to her. "You're not doing drugs, are you?"

"Mom! No! What's the matter with you?"

"Well, what am I supposed to think? In the past couple of months you've turned into a person I hardly recognize." She sighed and patted my shoulder. "It's just that you've worked so hard this year to get your grades up and keep up with your work at the paper. It's important for getting into college. I don't want you to lose it now."

"I won't. But I need a break. I haven't missed a single day of school all year."

That was the one small point of pride I had left, the thing I still gave myself credit for. But today I couldn't take it.

Mom raked a hand through her hair. "I suppose one afternoon won't hurt anything. You can start on your sophomore reading list. I'm sure I have a copy of *Silas Marner* around here somewhere."

Trying to make sense of the train wreck my life had become, I filled up three pages in the brown leather journal I had started last year, then spent the rest of the afternoon skimming the novel and memorizing my lines for the production of *Romeo and Juliet*, which was now just weeks away. Ms. Costello had decided that dress rehearsal would be open to the whole school. Camilla and I were supposed to toss another coin to see who would narrate at the rehearsal, but I was already planning to be sick that day to avoid being heckled in front of everybody.

After dinner that night Dad insisted we go to a movie. I sat behind him and Mom in the darkened theater, eating a jumbo box of Junior Mints and only half listening to the prissy British costume drama unfolding on the screen.

The next day at school was a carbon copy of all the others, except for a fire drill after third period, a food fight that erupted when the cafeteria ran out of nachos, and the fact that Ms. Costello was not in her classroom when we showed up for Shakespeare that afternoon. Miss Morrison, a shy student teacher from across the hall, came into the room and folded her hands, waiting quietly for our attention. A classic rookie mistake. People went on with their conversations, totally ignoring her, until Sabrina finally took pity on the clueless Miss M. and said, "Quiet, everybody! The baby teacher wants to talk."

"Ms. Costello went to pick up your costumes and has been caught in traffic downtown," Miss Morrison said. "She'll be here in a few minutes. Until then you are to remain here and study your lines. I'll be right across the hall if you need anything."

She checked the class roll, then caught my eye and said, "Would you please take the attendance slip to the office?"

When I got back from the office, I heard laughter even before I went inside.

"'. . . never dreamed a first kiss could be so perfect as it was with Jason,'" Camilla read in an overly breathy voice. Everybody snickered. My face flamed.

"Give me that!" I reached for my journal, but Camilla snatched it away. "'That's why getting dumped hurts so bad—to know he didn't really mean it.'" She grinned at me. "Poor baby. Did she get her feelings hurt?"

"Shut *up*, Camilla! Give me my journal."

Instead she tossed it to Sabrina, who gave me a pitying look before tossing it back to Camilla.

Camilla flipped the pages. "Oh, here's a juicy passage. "'February tenth. Gave my number to some totally geeky guy at the movies. Don't know why except maybe I want so bad to matter to somebody. Since Jason, I feel like nobody will ever want me.'"

Then Ryan Adams, who was playing Romeo opposite Sabrina, pretended to swoon and said, "Oh, woe is me! My grave is like to be my wedding bed!"

The whole class howled. I wanted to die. I grabbed for my journal again just as Camilla jerked her arm away, the classroom door opened, and Ms. Costello staggered in beneath a stack of boxes from the Ridgeview Costume Shoppe.

"Ms. Costello!" Camilla whined, sounding like a second grader who had been horribly wronged. "Haley Patterson just ripped my brand-new shirt."

Frowning, Miss Costello set the boxes on the floor. "Haley? What's going on?"

I was on the floor putting my stuff back into my backpack. "She stole my journal. I want it back."

"Well, why don't you just ask her for it?"

Gee. Why didn't I think of that?

"Here!" Camilla tossed my journal onto the floor. "It's boring as dirt anyway."

Ms. Costello glanced at her watch. "There isn't enough time to run lines today. Let's try on these costumes and go over the cast lists. Remember, it's the responsibility of the Friday night cast to be sure the Saturday night people have the costumes in plenty of time for curtain."

Camilla tried on the costume we were to share for our role as narrator. It was a pale ivory thing with extra-wide long sleeves and a fringed, rope-like gold belt that looked like the tiebacks on Mom's dining room drapes.

"Ms. Costello," Camilla said, tossing her blond mane. "Perhaps you didn't notice, but I am a size zero. This costume is miles and miles too big for me."

"It's fine, Camilla," Miss Costello said. "Just cinch the waist a little more."

"But I look like a sack of potatoes!" Camilla complained. "Can't we exchange it for a smaller size?"

"Haley has to wear it, too," Ms. Costello said.

"Oh, right," Camilla muttered. "I forgot I have to share with the hippo."

She stepped out of the costume and tossed it to me, but before I could try it on, the bell rang. I grabbed my stuff and left. Camilla followed me into the hallway and up the stairs to my locker. There, protected by the crush of people heading to seventh-period classes, she jabbed me in the ribs so hard my eyes watered. "That's for ripping my shirt. Don't do it again."

"Camilla?" The principal was coming toward us. Maybe he'd seen what she did and justice would prevail after all.

"Yes, sir?"

I dug through my locker looking for my history book, waiting for the throbbing pain in my ribs to go away. Above the noise of the hallway Mr. Parsons said, "The school board wants to print up a new brochure for prospective students, and Miss Brinkley thinks you'd be the perfect person for the cover."

I slammed my locker shut and pushed past them just as Camilla flashed her superdiva smile and said, "Gosh, Mr. Parsons. I'd be honored."

Two weeks later Ms. Costello reminded me that because Camilla was posing for brochure pictures on Friday, the role of the narrator for the dress rehearsal was all mine. Like that was a big prize I really wanted.

That afternoon I stood onstage in that flimsy costume, introducing the two lovers from Verona to an audience who couldn't have cared less. They were just happy to get out of their last-period classes. Maybe it was the novelty of the scenery and the costumes, or maybe people were just tired, but for whatever reason I got through my part without much trouble. At the end of the play I took my bow with the rest of the cast. Patrick was in the front row with a couple of people from the paper and several other seniors, clapping for me, and I thought that just maybe my long nightmare was over.

Friday night I skipped the performance and stayed home in my pajamas, watching *Star Trek* reruns and eating cold pizza while Mom and Dad went to a faculty to-do at the university. The next night I got to school a half hour early and went to the makeshift dressing room next to the library to get the costume back from the superdiva.

Who was nowhere to be found. Sabrina and Ryan were already in their costumes and stage makeup, running their lines. Sandi, who had a small role as Juliet's nurse, was standing in the corner, mouthing her lines to herself.

"Sandi. Have you seen Camilla? I need my costume."

"Why ask me?" Sandi turned away and resumed her muttering.

"Sabrina!" I grabbed her arm as she rushed toward the wings. "Where's Camilla? She has my costume!"

"Haven't seen her. I gotta go." Sabrina waved one hand. "There's Ms. Costello. Ask her."

Ms. Costello rushed toward me. "Haley! Why aren't you dressed? Curtain is in ten minutes."

"I can't find Camilla. She has the costume."

"Are you sure she hasn't already give it to you?"

Are you sure you are not a total moron?

"I wasn't here last night. I haven't seen Camilla all day."

Then Camilla made a grand entrance and shoved the costume into my hands. When she realized Ms. Costello was standing right there, she muttered, "Sorry I'm late."

"Never mind that," Ms. Costello said. "Hurry up, Haley. Get dressed."

I ran for the dressing room, shucked out of my jeans and shirt and pulled the costume over my head. Then I noticed a huge tear down the side.

I ran out of the room, holding the costume closed with one hand and ran straight into Camilla. She crossed her arms and smiled. "Is there a problem?"

"What is it, Haley?" Ms. Costello asked.

"The costume is ripped."

"How did *that* happen?"

Camilla's eyes widened. "It was perfect when I gave it to her. She must have caught it on a nail or something."

"Never mind." Ms. C rummaged in her bag for a couple of safety pins. She pinned the costume closed and draped the fabric to one side. "There. No one will notice. Now hurry, the music is starting."

I followed Ms. Costello to the dimly lit wings and waited for my cue. Camilla brushed past me on the way to her seat. "Now we're even, Patterson. Break a leg."

The curtain rose. I walked to center stage, to the X marked with blue tape, and looked past the footlights at the upturned faces in the first row and the darkness beyond. I imagined hundreds of pairs of eyes staring at my damaged costume, and I totally blanked.

The theater was pin-drop quiet. My heart thudded wildly in my chest. What were my first lines?

"Two households!" Ms. Costello hissed from the wings. "Both alike in dignity . . ."

And my brain switched on. "Two households," I began, my voice wobbly with relief, "both alike in dignity, in fair Verona, where we lay our scene . . . a pair of star-cross'd lovers take their life . . ."

And the play went on. Once, Sabrina forgot her lines when a baby in the audience started to cry, and near the end Alex Parker, who was playing the role of the friar, tripped on the hem of his costume. But eventually it was time for my final lines.

"The sun for sorrow will not show his head," I recited. "Go hence, to have more talk of these sad things; some shall be pardon'd, and some punished: For never was a story of more woe than this of Juliet and her Romeo."

Applause rippled across the auditorium. The cast held hands and took a bow as the lights came up. Sabrina's dad strode to the front of the stage and handed her an armload of red roses, which made the applause start all over again.

Backstage, Ms. Costello was beaming. "Great job, everyone! Cast party at my house in half an hour. Anyone need a ride?"

People started forming car pools, but I slipped away to the dressing room and changed out of the ruined costume. I was sure I'd have to pay for the damage, but I was so glad to have the play over with that I didn't even care.

In the parking lot Mom and Dad congratulated me on a fine performance, and I thanked them, even though I had begged them not to come. Dad started the car. In the glow of the headlights I saw Sabrina, Ryan, and Alex climbing into a car with Camilla.

"Aren't you going to the cast party?" Mom asked.

"I'm tired. I just want to crash." I opened the car door.

"Oh, but honey, going the cast party is one of the best parts of being in a play. Don't you want to stop by, even for a little while? Daddy or I will pick you up."

Dad said, "It's no big deal, Carol. If she's too tired, I don't think we ought to push her."

"Fine." We got into the car and Mom fastened her seat belt. "I just worry about her is all," she said, as if I weren't there. "She lives like a hermit."

Somehow I got through the last miserable days, past final exams and the checking in of books and equipment. Yearbook day, which was the day of the annual slide show, was one of the worst. People were rushing around, writing immortal prose in each other's books, signing their pictures. Nobody was asking for my autograph, and I wasn't about to ask for theirs and risk rejection. During the open period I wandered out to the quad and sat on the concrete bench, my knees drawn up to my chest.

"Can I have your autograph?" Patrick asked, sliding onto the bench beside me.

"Are you sure Catherine won't mind? After all, I'm such a horrible person I might contaminate your whole year-book, and then where would you be?"

"You were a part of my staff this year," Patrick said. "Someday, when you're writing for the *New York Times*, I want to be able to prove I knew you back in high school."

"Yeah, right."

"It could happen. You're talented, Haley. Mrs. Westfall knows that. So even if you don't get the byline next year, you have to stay on staff." He handed me his pen and his yearbook, which was open to the photo of the whole *Review* staff taken in September. Maddie and Simone had already added their signatures; Simone had dotted the *i* in her name with a tiny little heart. I signed my name. Then I scribbled, "Thanks," and handed it back.

The bell rang, and we went inside the auditorium to the slide show. Maddie, Flip, and the rest of the staffers staked out a row of seats near the back. Patrick sat in a special section down front that had been reserved for graduating seniors, the seats decorated with red and white ribbons. I hunched in my seat on the aisle across from Mrs. Westfall.

Mr. Parsons stepped to the mike and congratulated us on completing a fine, fine year at RHS, then turned the mike over to Mr. Rathburn, the yearbook advisor, who introduced his staff and told us how hard they'd worked to produce a yearbook we'd cherish forever. The show began. The pictures were arranged in chronological order, starting with the annual Howdy Dance in September and moving on through homecoming, the sports seasons, the winter formal, and the prom. There were pictures of club members, and a shot of Mr. Rathburn and some of the other teachers dressed in Halloween costumes. A picture of Camilla, taken at a midyear cheerleading clinic, flashed onto the screen. People clapped and cheered. A couple of guys whistled.

A shot of the basketball team appeared, and a bunch of guys yelled, "Woo-hoo! Raiders rule!" Then the picture of the *Review* staff taken back in September, the same one in the yearbook, came up. My stomach clenched. A few people clapped. Some of the seniors yelled, "Yea, Patrick!" Then Jason the Jerk hollered, "There's Patterson!" and several boys made loud kissing noises that made everyone laugh.

I ran out of the auditorium. Mrs. Westfall caught up with me in the restroom. "Come on, Haley. They didn't mean it. It's typical year-end craziness. Kids blowing off steam. You can't let it get to you."

I folded my arms across my chest. "I'm not going back in there."

She sighed and scribbled a hall pass for me, and I waited out the rest of the slide show in the guidance office.

\\||||/

On the next-to-last Friday of the school year the final edition of the *Review* came out. The following week, seniors skipped classes on Senior Day, and Mr. Parsons handed out a bunch of awards during the last assembly of the year. I sat by myself at the back of the auditorium working a crossword puzzle while Suzanne accepted a certificate for earning all As, Camilla claimed the cheerleaders' Spirit Award, and Vanessa got a certificate and a plaque for winning a couple of art competitions. The only surprise was when Sandi Ahrens won the award for Best Performance for her tiny part in *Romeo and Juliet*, an award everyone had expected Sabrina to win.

Finally it was over. On Memorial Day I started packing for my summer at Aunt Bitsy's. I was folding a cotton sweater when the doorbell rang.

"Here," Suzanne said when I opened the door. She thrust a silver and white striped shopping bag filled with CDs, nail polish, and a hairstyle magazine into my hands. "You left this at my house. After Vanessa's birthday party."

Tears welled in my eyes. Vanessa's party had been a blast. Now it seemed like something I'd seen on TV, something that had happened to someone else.

"I'm surprised you didn't trash my stuff, the way you've trashed my whole life."

I started to close the door, but Suzanne held it open. "Look, Haley. Try to understand."

"Oh, I understand. You let Camilla ruin my life and never once stood up for me. I'll never forgive you."

"You think you are such hot stuff because you're the only freshman on the paper. As if anybody cares."

"You're *jealous* because I got some attention for once?"

"Jealous? Of Patrick and Maddie and that whole bunch of geeky losers? Don't make me laugh."

"I thought you were proud of me. I thought we were friends."

"Yeah," Suzanne said, "I thought so, too. But what you did to me is proof that you never really cared about me."

"I said I was sorry. What else can I do?"

"I have to go."

"So go. I'm not stopping you."

"And one more thing," Suzanne said, stepping away from the door. "You can forget about my coming up to Copper Springs this summer. You can rot up there for all I care."

"Fine!" I slammed the door and leaned against it, tears streaming down my face.

The phone in the kitchen rang, and I picked it up.

"Hey, kid," said my brother. "What's going on?"

"Peyton! Where are you?"

"Rome. But me and a couple of the guys are heading for Venice."

My nose started to run. I grabbed a paper towel and wiped my face. "Sounds great."

"You don't sound so great, though. What's the matter?"

I didn't feel like spilling my guts to Peyton; he was never much help in a crisis, and besides, what could he do from five thousand miles away? "I'm okay. Packing for Aunt Bitsy's. Dad is driving me up there on Thursday."

"Is he home?"

"Nope. He and Mom are at some event downtown. It's Memorial Day."

"That's right. I forgot."

In the background I heard a couple of guys laughing, calling his name, and then Peyton said, "Listen, I'm about to miss my train. Tell Mom and Dad I called, will you? Tell them I'll call from Venice in a couple of days."

"Okay."

"And Haley? Don't be so glum. It's true there isn't much to do in Copper Springs, but Aunt B is basically cool. And you can always hang out at her country club and work on your tan. Catch you later, kid. Bye!"

On Thursday, as we drove to Copper Springs, Dad and I talked about the series of editorials he'd finished writing, and about his plans to see every museum in England while Mom taught her classes.

"It's exhausting just thinking of it," Dad said as the

scenery flowed past, "but your mother is excited. And the change will do me good. We haven't taken a real vacation in a while." He glanced over at me. "You and I are both so intense, Haley. We need to pace ourselves. You know what I mean?"

Tired of having to hold up my end of the conversation, I nodded and kept my eyes on the ribbon of road taking us higher into the cool, pine-scented mountains.

By three o'clock we were entering Copper Springs, an old resort town with rows of restored Victorian houses that had been turned into shops and tea rooms for tourists. Except for a new green and gold welcome sign, the town looked exactly the same as it had on our last visit to Aunt Bitsy's a couple of summers before. Dad slowed as we drove past souvenir shops, a drugstore, a couple of art galleries, and an old redbrick mansion that had been converted into a museum. Tourists wearing flip-flops, T-shirts, and fanny packs, their digital cameras dangling from around their necks, waited for rides at the amusement park, where an antique carousel was the main attraction.

"Just like old times, isn't it?" Dad braked for a family with three little kids who were jaywalking across the street. "Remember the year Bitsy let you ride with her in the Independence Day parade?"

"Yeah. I loved having an aunt who was mayor."

As Dad made the turn onto Pinecrest Drive, I saw Aunt Bitsy's yellow house nestled among a stand of pines at the top of the hill. When I was younger, I'd spent hours in the tree house in her backyard. From there you could see all the way across town to the rooftops of the resort cabins, the dance pavilion, and farther out, the pewter-colored water of Mirror Lake. Dad pulled into the driveway and honked the horn.

Aunt B rushed out, the sleeves of her gauzy yellow smock billowing out behind her. We got out of the car and she threw herself into Dad's arms. "Freddie!"

"Hi, Bits. How are you?" Dad kissed her cheek and drew back to look down at her.

"Oh, mean as ever." She let Dad go and hugged me. "Haley, darling, I can't believe how grown up you are!"

"Hi, Aunt B."

Dad unlocked the car trunk. Aunt Bitsy fluttered around us like an exotic little bird. "Careful now, Freddie, don't hurt your back. You know how you always overdo."

I grabbed my duffel bag. Dad unloaded my suitcases and the tote bag full of books Mom had insisted I bring so I could keep up with my summer reading.

Aunt Bitsy flapped her hand at me. "Now, Haley, darling, you just go right on in, but watch that second step; there's a loose board and I haven't had time to fix it. Freddie, take her things up to the front bedroom, the one with the pink wallpaper, and I'll meet you in the kitchen. I made lunch."

While we ate, Dad filled Aunt B in on his and Mom's plans for England. I updated her on Peyton's travels and told her about the competition for the byline at the *Review*. I speared a forkful of spinach salad. "But the winner won't be announced until fall."

"Well, if you don't win," my aunt declared, "it only proves the judges are stupid." She buttered a piece of bread. "I still have those clippings your mother sent, from back in February, I believe it was. That piece you wrote about the effects of grade inflation on college freshmen was nothing short of brilliant." She grinned. "And the gossip column was fun too."

Not for me.

"Haley?" Dad said. "You're a million miles away."

"Sorry." I blinked back tears and sipped my tea. "I was thinking about the contest."

Finally Dad said, "I hate to eat and run, but it's a long drive back, and Carol and I have to be at the airport in Denver extra early tomorrow. Security checks take forever now."

"Tell me about it," Aunt Bitsy said. "Those new precautions are such a headache, and I for one do not feel one bit safer. All they do is slow people down. Here I am, sixty years old, and last month they made me take off my shoes *and* my jacket, they threw away a perfectly good tube of toothpaste and my favorite shampoo, and then some gum-chewing Amazon in a tacky uniform grabbed my bosom, searching for bombs in my underwire bra! The next thing you know, we'll all be flying stark naked."

Dad grinned. "That should certainly cut down on the number of passengers."

"You're laughing," Aunt B said darkly, "but you just wait."

We walked out to the car. Dad hugged me. "Have

a great summer, honey. We'll call you from London."

He backed down the drive, tooted the horn, and was gone.

"I'm glad you're here." Aunt Bitsy draped her arm around my shoulders. "It has been way too long since we had a real visit. What would you like to do this afternoon?"

"I don't know."

"We could swim at my country club, or go shopping, although most of the stuff for sale around here is tourist junk made in China. They're about to take over the world, you know."

"Tourists?"

"The Chinese! I was reading in the paper just the other day that some big Chinese conglomerate wants to take over an American washing-machine company. Who would have ever thought that could happen?"

Then I remembered why I always came home from Aunt Bitsy's feeling exhausted. Her mind was so nimble, jumping from one idea to the next, it was hard to keep up. Now she said, "I know! I'll take you down to my shop."

Aunt B was always involved in something—a community blood drive, a local election, the annual arts fair downtown—but this was the first I'd heard of a commercial enterprise.

"It's just a little one," Aunt B continued. "I had to do something with my time after my two terms as mayor ran out. A person can watch only so much TV before brain rot sets in."

She was already heading back inside, picking up her

keys, pawing through a huge straw bag for her sunglasses. "We'll pop in for a little while and then I'll take you to Pirate's Cove for dinner. They just put wild salmon back on the menu."

After my huge lunch I didn't even want to think about another meal, but I followed her to the garage. She punched the button and the door opened to reveal a sparkling red convertible.

"That's the parade car!" I said. "The one we rode in on the Fourth of July."

"Yep." She slid behind the wheel. "I sweet-talked Arlen Hooper into letting me have it at a good price. It's practically an antique now, but it still runs like a top. Jump in!"

I got in, and she sped back down Pinecrest and onto the main road. The tourist crowd was thinning; people were packing up kids and cameras, thinking about where to go for dinner.

Aunt B pulled into a parking space outside a pale blue Victorian-style building. A sign above the door said BACK IN THYME. And down below, in smaller letters: OLD-FASHIONED HERBAL REMEDIES FOR MODERN-DAY MALADIES. ELIZABETH PATTERSON, PROPRIETOR. On the doorknob was another sign that said CLOSED. PLEASE CALL AGAIN.

She unlocked the door, flipped the sign to the OPEN side, and switched on the light. The shop was decorated like an old-fashioned parlor, with two red velvet chairs facing a fireplace. A stack of books and a vase of summer flowers sat on a polished tea table. Shelves filled with jars of dried grasses and withered berries lined three walls. I read the labels: lavender, cat's claw, feverfew, chen pi, and on around the room to aloe, milk thistle, motherwort, and saw palmetto. A fat pumpkin-colored cat emerged from behind the old-fashioned cash register and jumped lightly to the floor.

Aunt Bitsy set her purse down and nudged him aside with her foot. "There you are, Bill. I knew you'd show up when you got hungry."

She reached under the counter and took out a bowl filled with something that smelled like a combination of week-old trout and rubber tires. "Dried tuna with herbs," she said. "It's my own secret recipe."

Bill sniffed, raised his tail, and walked away.

"He's holding out for that canned stuff, but it's bad for him. He has kidney problems." She waved a hand toward the back of the shop. "My herb garden is out back. I grow almost all my own stuff. Do you know how to work a cash register?"

"What?"

"It isn't hard. This one is like me, old and temperamental, but I wouldn't trade it for half a dozen of those computerized ones." She rushed on. "We're open from ten to five, except for Thursdays when we're open till seven. Saturdays we close at noon. Of course I don't expect you to work here all the time. You *are* on summer vacation after all, but it's better to have some structure in the day. Rather than sitting around in one's pajamas till all hours."

Wait! I wanted to yell. *Who said anything about my working all summer? What if I want to spend all day in front of the TV letting my brain rot?*

The bell over the door tinkled as a blond woman came in with a pink-faced, runny-nosed kid. Some kind of red liquid had spilled and dried on his shirt. Both his shoes were untied.

"Thank goodness you're open," the woman said to my aunt. "We just arrived, and Harold is coming down with a cold. If he gets sick, our whole vacation will be ruined! Do you have anything to ward it off?"

Aunt Bitsy flew into action. "Echinacea," she said. "And raspberry bark tea. Haley darling, get the step stool and hand me that blue bottle on the top shelf."

I got the bottle for her. She poured a couple of white tablets into a mortar and started grinding them. "Look in that basket next to the cash register and get that plastic bag. Now open it up and dump it in here."

I opened the bag and a cloud of fine brown dust filled the air. My nose prickled. I sneezed.

"Bless you," the woman said.

"Bless you!" yelled Harold.

"Thanks." A balloon had suddenly inflated inside my head, cutting off my oxygen. I dropped the plastic bag onto the counter. "Excuse me."

I ran outside. My eyes burned. My skin began to itch. I scratched my arms until a bumpy red rash appeared. The woman came out of the shop with her packages. Harold trailed behind her, licking a peppermint sucker.

Aunt Bitsy came outside, took one look at me and said, "Uh-oh."

"Wad?"

"Allergic reaction. It happens to some people." Then she saw the rash on my arms. "This could be serious. Let's get you to the doctor."

Fifteen minutes later we were ushered into the doctor's office. He peered at me over his half-moon glasses and said mine was one of the worst allergic reactions he'd ever seen. He gave me a shot, a cream for the prickly rash on my arm, and a warning to stay away from Back in Thyme.

Aunt B drove me straight home and put me to bed. "Get some rest, and don't worry about a thing. Obviously working at the shop this summer is totally out of the question, but never mind. I have a plan!"

After the long drive from Ridgeview, too much food, Aunt B's manic activity, and the allergy shot, I was totally wiped out.

"Wadever."

I pulled the sheet over my head.

Chapter Four

After my allergies calmed down, I told Aunt Bitsy I'd had a hard year at school and I just wanted to veg for a while—but no. She had decided that working at the Copper Springs Resort would be good for me, and once she makes up her mind about something she's like a runaway train, and there is nothing to do but hold on and ride it out.

Mr. Porter, the tubby, balding hiring manager, asked me a bazillion questions, then leaned back, folded his hands across his stomach, and smiled benignly, like the golden Buddha in my world-history textbook.

"Normally we don't hire anyone under age sixteen," he said, as if he were doing me the world's biggest favor, "but you seem responsible and level-headed. And your aunt vouches for you. Elizabeth Patterson's word counts for a lot around here."

"Yes, sir." I smoothed a wrinkle out of my denim skirt.

He flipped through a stack of papers on his desk. "We have an opening at the pool house. You'll be handing out towels for our guests, taking the used ones to the laundry, and selling sodas and ice cream. And keeping an eye on the lost and found. Think you can handle it?"

"Yes, sir."

He handed me a sheet of paper. "Staff orientation starts tomorrow at nine a.m. sharp. You'll need some khaki shorts, white sneakers, and white crew socks. We'll supply your shirts. We open on Tuesday morning."

He stood up and we shook hands across his desk. "Welcome aboard."

"Thank you." I folded the paper, tucked it into my purse, and headed for the door.

Just as I got there, he said, "Haley?"

I turned around.

"People on vacation like to see happy people wherever they go. Could you maybe smile now and then?"

I gave him my most dazzling TV model smile.

"Perfect." He waved one pudgy hand and went back to his stack of papers. "See you tomorrow. Don't be late."

Aunt Bitsy was waiting for me in the parking lot. The convertible's top was down, and some ancient Motown song was blasting through the speakers.

"Hi, sweetie."

I got into the car and dug my sunglasses out of my bag. "How did it go?"

I shrugged. I was still halfway mad that I'd been forced

into working when all I wanted to do was hole up in my room and figure out how to get my life back. "I have to buy khaki shorts and stuff. I'm going to work at the pool house."

"That's good," she said, throwing the car into reverse. "You'll meet some nice young people at the pool. You'll get to know everybody."

Which was precisely what I feared most. How could I protect myself when I wasn't even sure who I was anymore? "I hate khaki," I said, partly because it was true, but mostly because I was in a crabby mood.

After lunch at the Italian place down the street from Back in Thyme, we drove to Pinehurst, where I stocked up on shorts, sneakers, and socks. On the way out of the mall we passed a hair salon, and Aunt B stopped suddenly. "I have a great idea! Why don't we get new hairstyles? I'm due for a cut, and I think you'd look cute with a—"

"No!" The word came out more harshly than I intended. But my hair was my security blanket, a thick brown curtain shielding me from view, shutting out everything.

Aunt Bitsy blinked. "I just thought . . . but never mind."

"Sorry. I'm nervous about the new job."

"How hard can it be?" She dug her keys out of her bag. "You'll be fine."

Aunt B dropped me at home and went to check on things at Back in Thyme. I opened a can of soda and went out to the back porch with my copy of *Silas Marner*, but I couldn't concentrate. I imagined Suzanne and Vanessa lying in the sun out at the lake, sharing secrets and planning sophomore year without one single thought of me. Romances blooming and fading against a backdrop of hot music and cool drinks, and the heady scent of suntan lotion hanging the air. I felt like a character in a science fiction novel, stopped cold by an invisible force field while the rest of the world went on around me.

The next morning Aunt B dropped me at the main entrance to the resort. A hand-lettered sign pointed the way to staff orientation.

"Hi!" A girl in red shorts and a white top met me at the door and handed me a folder and a number-two pencil. "I'm Cindy." She consulted her clipboard. "And you are?"

"Haley Patterson."

She checked my name off her list. "Sit anywhere. We'll get started soon. There's OJ and doughnuts, if you're hungry."

I grabbed a doughnut and read through the folder, which contained a history of the Copper Springs Resort, a list of nearby attractions, and "Ten Rules for Staff Conduct." (Number one: Smile!)

The door opened, and in walked a seriously overweight girl wearing tight white capri pants, high-heeled sandals, and a pullover top with red and white horizontal stripes, thereby breaking every fashion rule I'd tried to live by in an effort to minimize the appearance of my hippo butt.

Someone sitting behind me yelled, "Frankie's back!" and a bunch of people surged toward her, laughing and jostling for hugs.

Cindy stepped up to the podium and tapped the mike. "Good morning."

"Good morning!" several people answered.

Cindy smiled. "That's what I like to see, people. Plenty of enthusiasm." She turned to Frankie, who was standing quietly to the side, flanked by a messy-haired boy with a goatee and a tall girl with straight honey-blond hair and thin wire-rimmed glasses. "Now that Frankie has arrived, we all have a reason to go on."

Everybody clapped. A couple of the guys hooted as Frankie made an exaggerated bow. She and her entourage took their seats.

For the next couple of hours Cindy led us through the endless information in our employee packets and walked us through a bunch of forms we had to complete in order to get paid. Once those were collected, she gave us a tour of the amphitheater, the pool, the tennis courts, the golf clubhouse, the dining room, and the riding stables. She handed out our work schedules. I would be working from nine to two every Monday, Wednesday, Friday, and Sunday. I'd have Tuesdays, Thursdays, and Saturdays free, except for the twice-monthly Saturday night movies, when all the staff were expected to show up.

Cindy told us where to pick up our shirts and employee name tags, answered a couple of questions, and said, "Lunch is ready in the main dining room. Enjoy your meal, and report to your supervisors at one thirty sharp. Any more questions?"

When no one spoke, she waved, and everyone headed

for the dining room. I hung back, letting the others go first, but after a while there was nothing to do but get in line.

"First year here?" asked the thin blonde with the funky glasses, the president of the Frankie Fan Club. I nodded.

"I'm Nora," she said. "Don't let the old-timers intimidate you. Most of them are really nice, but the first few days here can be overwhelming."

"Thanks."

She peered at me though her glasses. "Do you have a name?"

"Haley."

"Cool," Nora said. "I'm never going to forgive my mother for naming me Nora. It's a throwback to Nora Charles, a character in a nineteen-thirties detective series who wore satin evening gowns and a diamond bracelet and went around sipping cocktails and solving murders. Like that would really happen."

We reached the serving line. Nora handed me a plate and a napkin with silverware rolled up inside and continued her lecture. "Some of the old movies are good, though. Wait until we start movie nights here at the resort. The staff take turns dressing up like the characters in the films. We act as ushers and hand out programs and popcorn. It's lame, but the guests get a real kick out of it."

She helped herself to enough food to feed an army, including a couple of different kinds of salad, fried chicken, green beans, mashed potatoes, and pecan pie. Everything looked delicious, but it was chock-full of calories and way off-limits for girls with butts like mine. I took an apple and a bottle of water.

Nora peered at my plate in horror. "That's all you're having?"

"I'm not hungry."

"Wait till you've spent a few days busting your behind to please the guests," Nora said. "You'll be hungry enough to eat the tablecloth."

"Nora!" Frankie waved from her crowded table across the room, and Nora said, "Come on. I'll introduce you to the queen bee."

She led me to the table and bumped Frankie with her hip. "Scoot over. We need two places here."

Frankie slid over and we sat down. Nora waved her hand. "Frankie, meet Haley. Haley, this is Frankie. Let's eat."

Up close, Frankie was beautiful. Clear blue eyes and the kind of peaches and cream complexion usually found only in magazines, plus a deep dimple when she smiled. She wore an armload of beaded bracelets and a tiny gold ring above one eyebrow. She buttered a roll and said to me, "I haven't seen you around before."

"She's new," Nora said. "So be nice to her."

I sipped my water.

Frankie chewed and swallowed. "Where are you from?"

"Ridgeview."

"Wow. You're a long way from home."

Nora set down her drumstick and nudged Frankie. "It's not that far. What are you trying to do, make her homesick?"

I looked around, feeling like a tourist observing a foreign

culture. Unlike high school, where certain cliques make it obvious who's popular and who's not, everybody here seemed to be totally into each other. I halfway expected the entire staff to break into a spontaneous rendition of "Kumbayah."

A tall blonde wearing pink shorts, a white tank top, and a killer tan hurried to a table near the back door and plopped her tray down just as a dark-haired girl with a camera slung around her neck jumped up and threw herself into the blonde's arms. They stood there with their heads touching, giggling and swaying together, their arms around each other's shoulders.

Nora grinned. "Melanie and Phoebe have arrived. Now life can begin."

Frankie waved her fork toward the two girls and filled me in. "The blonde is Melanie Foster. She runs the kiddie theater class. Her grandmother is Opal Hubbard, the Broadway actress. The other one is Phoebe . . . something. Anyway, they're both from Texas, but they met here last year and got to be best buds. You hardly ever see one without the other."

Nora salted her mashed potatoes. "So, Haley, where are you working?"

"The pool house."

"You're kidding!" one of the other girls cried. "You get to work with Evan! This is my second year here, and I'm dying to work there, but Mr. Porter won't let me."

"That's why," Nora said. She looked at Frankie. "Are you going to eat that last roll?"

"Be my guest." Frankie handed it over.

"Why what?" the girl said.

"Mr. Porter knows you're nuts about our hunky life-guard, so that's why he won't let you work together." Nora buttered her roll. "People would drown while you two made goo-goo eyes at each other, and dead guests are bad for business."

Frankie polished off a piece of chocolate cake and glanced at her watch. "Yikes! Time to go!"

We cleared the table. As I was stacking my plate in the rubber bin, Frankie and Nora came up to me. Standing side by side, Nora tall and angular, Frankie round as a peach, they resembled the number 10.

"We're going to the pavilion tonight," Frankie said. "It's our last chance to kick back before the first guests arrive. You should come with us and meet everybody."

"It'll be fun," Nora said. "You'll get to know people before we get too busy."

When I was a little kid visiting Aunt Bitsy, I couldn't wait to grow up and hang out at the pavilion. Late at night I'd sneak outside to the tree house. From there I could see the twinkling lights reflecting on the dark water and hear music and laughter twining through the trees. But now I felt like a wounded animal, trying to survive by staying quiet and out of sight.

"I can't," I told Nora.

I left the dining hall and made my way to the pool house—and Evan.

Chapter Five

He stood with his back to the door, counting towels and muttering to himself.

"Excuse me," I said.

Evan turned around, and I saw why the girl at the lunch table had been so eager to work with him: If you looked in the dictionary under "gorgeous," there would be his picture staring back at you. Blue eyes, dark curly hair, a killer smile. Definitely number one on any girl's speed dial. He leaned against the door frame with the casual confidence some guys are born with, and folded his arms.

"What can I do for you?"

"I'm supposed to work here. In the pool house."

"Oh, right!" He picked up a clipboard and scanned a list. "Holly?"

"Haley."

"You look awfully young."

But inside I feel about a thousand years old. "I'll turn fifteen in a few weeks."

"Wow. Fifteen."

I couldn't tell whether he was trying to be friendly or making fun of me. He scribbled on a sheet of paper attached to a clipboard. "Most people who work here are at least sixteen. How'd you get in?"

"My aunt Bitsy lives here. I'm staying with her this summer."

"Lots of people have relatives here. What's so special about you?"

Nothing. Nothing at all. "You want to show me what I'm supposed to do?"

He unlatched a little gate that separated the towel area from the counter and waved me inside. "This is where we keep the fresh towels. Be sure the shelves are full at all times. The used ones go into those big plastic bins over there." He jerked his thumb toward a corner. "When the bins get full, roll them to the laundry and pick up a fresh batch. The check-out sheets are on the clipboard. Write down each guest's name and room number when they check the towels out, and cross them off when they return them. Any that go missing are replaced out of your paycheck, and they aren't cheap."

Just then a cute, if slightly scruffy blond-haired guy wearing flip-flops, loose cargo pants, and a faded concert T-shirt came in. "Hey, Evan? The delivery guys want to know where to put the pool chemicals."

"I'll be right there." Evan turned back to me. "The ice-cream freezer is under this counter. Soft-drink machine is behind you. Keep an eye on the ice machine and let someone know when it's half empty. People get all bent out of shape when there's no ice for their sodas."

Outside, a truck horn blared. Evan said, "Hang on a sec, and I'll show you how the cash register works."

He and Mr. Scruffy left, and I wandered around the small space, looking at the schedule posted on the wall, the dog-eared mystery novel lying on a shelf. Beneath the counter was a wire basket containing a bottle of suntan lotion, a silver whistle on a braided plastic cord, a pair of wrap-around sunglasses, and a set of car keys. Evan's personal stuff. Inside a cardboard box labeled LOST AND FOUND were a few leftovers from the previous summer: a pair of manicure scissors, a couple of pairs of sunglasses, and a copy of *War and Peace* marked up with hot-pink highlighter.

Outside, the pool sparkled in the sunlight. I could hear Evan and the blond guy laughing and talking to a delivery man as they placed huge containers of chlorine tablets in a storage shed behind the lifeguard chair. Evan signed a paper, the delivery man and Mr. Scruffy left, and Evan came back inside.

"So, Haley, any questions?"

"The cash register?"

"It's easy. Just scan the purchases and hit the total button. Most people pay with a special resort charge card, but if you get cash, it goes in the bottom of the drawer.

You have to balance the drawer at the beginning and end of every shift. You know how to do that, right?"

I had no clue, but Evan already thought I was a baby who didn't really belong there. "Sure," I said. "No problem."

"That's about it." He fished his keys and sunglasses out of the wire basket. "I've got to run over to the dining hall to post a list of water-aerobics classes. You need a ride?"

It was such a surprise after the chilly reception he'd given me that for a minute I couldn't say anything.

"It's not rocket science, Haley. You want to come or not?"

"That would be great."

"Okay. Let's roll."

We went out back and got into a Jeep with the resort's gold and green logo on the door. Evan started the engine, and we roared out of the parking lot and onto the narrow paved road that wound through the resort. Halfway to the dining hall we met a couple of girls in resort uniforms, heading for the tennis courts. Evan slowed and tapped the horn. The girls looked up. "Evan!" they squealed. "Hi!"

He stopped the Jeep. "How's it going, girls?"

"You know. Same old drag," said a tall redhead with a tennis racquet under her arm. "Another fascinating summer teaching tennis to nine-year-olds." She ducked her head, looked past Evan, and said, "Who's this?"

"Her name's Haley. She's the pool-house mascot this year."

"Hi," she said. "I'm Angie. You play tennis?"

"Not really." Sunlight bounced off the hood of the Jeep, practically blinding me.

"It's fun," she said. "Come around sometime and we'll show you the basics. Right, Joss?"

The other girl nodded. "Why not?"

Another Jeep pulled up behind us and Evan said, "We gotta go. See you."

We continued along the road. On the way to the dining hall Evan pointed out the places Cindy had shown us on the morning tour, but he added a bunch of details she had left out: Al Capone once visited the resort with three of his bodyguards, and he wouldn't eat any of the resort food for fear he'd be poisoned; a couple of college kids hiking in the mountains got lost and were rescued six days later; President Reagan once made a speech from the porch of the main building, and a crowd stood in the pouring rain to hear him. Back in the late 1800s a girl drowned in the dark waters near the pavilion, and some people said she still haunted the place.

"My aunt has lived here most of her life, and she never told me any of this," I said as the dining hall came into view through the trees.

"My great-grandfather helped build this place, and he still loves to talk about it. Here we are."

He parked the Jeep and took the flyers off the backseat. "I need to put these up, and then I'm heading back to the pool. I'll see you later."

Evan went inside the dining hall, and I waited in the parking lot for Aunt Bitsy to pick me up. Nora and Frankie rounded the corner. Spotting Evan's Jeep, Nora grinned.

"Nice going, Haley. You've already snagged the biggest heartthrob in the entire resort. No wonder you don't want to hang out with Frankie and me."

Frankie's beautiful blue eyes narrowed. "Watch out. He'll rip out your heart and stomp it flat as a dime."

"He thinks I'm a baby," I said. "A mascot! He isn't interested in me."

"Don't be so sure," Nora said.

Frankie tossed her thick braid. "So, you're all set for your first shift at the pool?"

"I guess so." I paused, wondering whether to trust them. Finally, I said, "How do you balance a cash drawer, anyway?"

"Uh-oh," Nora said. "Now you have to come with us tonight. We've got some major tutoring to do, girl."

A part of me wanted to hang out like a normal teenager and forget my troubles. But terror whispered in my ear that if Nora and Frankie found out who I really was—a beaten-down loser, a pathetic pariah who was too scared to stand up for herself—they'd hate me too.

"Never mind," I said. "My aunt owns a store. I'll ask her."

Frankie's face closed down. "Fine. Whatever. Come on, Nora."

Later Aunt Bitsy gave me a crash course in how to handle the cash flowing through the register, how to count the opening balance and reconcile it with the cash-register tape at the end of the day.

After supper I sat on the porch listening to the laughter and music coming from the pavilion. I heard the TV go off. The screen door squeaked open and Aunt B said, "Haley? I'm going to bed. Don't forget to lock the doors before you turn in."

I sat in the dark for a while longer, thinking about the train wreck that was my life. The long summer stretched ahead of me, but eventually I'd have to go back to school.

Up in my room I took out my cell, wanting more than anything to call Suzanne, but scared I'd start to cry, or that she'd hang up on me. I found a pen and ripped a sheet of paper out of my reporter's notebook.

Dear Suzanne, I began. *When I wrote that gossip piece about you and Sean Davis, I wasn't trying to hurt you. I can't believe that now you are using it as the reason for cutting me out of your life. Please . . .*

I stopped. It sounded all wrong. I started over. *Dear Suzanne, Please don't be mad at me about that Sean Davis thing. Nobody takes that column seriously. You are way too smart not to see that Camilla is just using it as an excuse to get back at me for reporting on her precious party and spoiling her trip.*

Wrong, wrong, wrong.

Aunt B knocked on my door. "Haley, are you still up?"

"Yeah."

She came into my room in her bathrobe and slippers, a couple of pink foam curlers in her hair. "It's nearly midnight, honey. Is anything wrong?"

"No, I'm good. Just winding down. You know."

"How about some hot cocoa? It might help you fall asleep."

"No, I'm okay."

"Don't stay up too late."

She closed the door and went down the hall to her room. Outside, the crickets and tree frogs sang. Wind rustled the tall pines. I took out another sheet of paper.

Dear Suzanne. Please.

Chapter Six

Wednesday morning. My first day at work. Aunt B dropped me at the resort entrance a few minutes before nine, and I headed down the paved trail to the pool house. Already the resort was filling up; cars and SUVs were parked in front of the rows of guest cabins scattered among the trees. Tennis balls thwacked against the courts, and through the open doorway of the spa I heard an aerobics instructor counting cadence.

Melanie, the blonde from Texas, was walking backward, leading a group of grade-school kids carrying costumes, and talking a mile a minute. "Today we'll practice reading our lines, okay? And tomorrow we'll learn the words to the songs," she said.

"I already know the words," one kid told her. "I got them on CD."

"Great." Melanie winked at me and waved as they headed for the amphitheater behind the dining hall.

Nora was standing on the back steps of the dining hall holding a clipboard, counting cartons of canned tomatoes and checking them off a list.

"Hi, Haley!" she caroled. "On your way to the pool?"

"Yeah."

"You're lucky," Nora said. "You'll get to meet loads of cool people. Meanwhile Frankie and I are stuck in the kitchen cracking eggs and chopping vegetables." She set the clipboard down and shaded her eyes with her hand.

"It wasn't my idea. My aunt made me take this job."

"Oh, you poor thing. Just think of how awful it's going to be, looking at cute guys in swim trunks all day while you fill their soft-drink cups. Such a hardship. I should call the child welfare people and have your mean old aunt arrested for cruelty."

I couldn't help smiling. "Okay, maybe it's not so bad."

"No kidding," Nora said. "You could have been assigned to mucking out the horses' stalls. Ugh."

"I like horses," I said, even though my experience with them was limited to summer camp back in fifth grade.

Nora waved her hand toward the stables. "The resort offers trail rides every day. You should sign up for one. You'll get an employee discount."

The door opened, and an enormous man in a chef's apron and a frizzy red ponytail came out. "Are you finished, Nora? If so, perhaps you'd like to cut your little party short and give Frankie a hand with the broccoli."

Behind his back Nora made a face and mouthed *broccoli*. She waggled her fingers at me, and I jogged the rest of the way to the pool house.

Where Evan stood, frowning. "It's five minutes past nine," he said when I hurried inside. "Just because your aunt is some big shot and they bent the rules for you doesn't give you the right to inconvenience everyone else."

He waved his hand toward the entrance to the pool, where a crowd of people clutching water toys and beach bags were waiting for the gates to open.

"I'm sorry. It won't happen again."

"It better not. I've counted the towels for you and checked the ice machine and the freezer. Think you can take it from here?"

"It's not exactly rocket science."

He grabbed his sunglasses, strode across the deck, and unlocked the gate. A bunch of kids made straight for the water, yelling and splashing with their toys. The adults, mostly women, settled into the lounge chairs arranged in a circle around the pool, donning sunglasses and smoothing on tanning lotion. Evan draped a whistle around his neck and climbed the metal ladder to the lifeguard tower at the far end of the pool. Someone turned on a boom box, and just like that, it was summer.

I sat on a wooden stool behind the counter, watching the kids play in the water. A couple of teenage girls came through the gate with all their stuff and settled into chairs across from Evan's lifeguard chair. One of them made a big show of taking off her T-shirt to reveal a tiny pink bikini. Then she looked up to see if Evan had noticed, but if he had, he didn't let on. He blew his whistle and motioned to two boys who were dunking each other near the diving board.

The clock hands inched toward ten. I was bored senseless. Then the door opened and a couple of eight-year-olds came in, dripping water onto the concrete floor.

One of them, a sandy-haired kid with freckles marching across his nose, asked, "You got any Red Bombers?"

I checked the freezer. "No Red Bombers, but there are Space Pops."

"Oh, I love Space Pops," said his friend. "Can I have a chocolate one?"

"I want chocolate too," said Freckles, handing me the Copper Springs Resort charge card.

I gave them their ice creams and swiped the card, and the cash register beeped.

They left, and another bunch came in for sodas and ice cream. I scanned purchases, made change, checked the ice machine, and wiped the sticky residue of a melting Space Pop off the counter. A couple of moms and the girl in the pink bikini came in to get towels, and before I knew it, the morning had passed.

Evan came in and grabbed a soda. "How's it going, Haley?"

"Okay."

"Are you hungry?"

"Starving."

"You can take an ice cream and soda if you want. Just be sure to write it down. Or you can wait till your shift ends and have lunch in the dining hall. The food isn't bad."

"Thanks."

The door to the service entrance opened, and the scruffy guy who had helped Evan unload the pool chemicals came in. Only today he didn't look quite so scruffy. His hair was pulled back into a short, neat ponytail. He wore jeans and a pair of scuffed brown boots. Aviator sunglasses dangled from the pocket of his faded black T-shirt, which said IMAGINE WHIRLED PEAS.

"I saw you here the other day," he said, leaning against the side of the counter. "When the chemicals came in?"

"I remember." His eyes were the deep blue of the ocean, and his teeth were very, very white.

"I'm Harrison Gray."

"Haley. Patterson." I wished he would quit looking at me. It made me nervous. "I'm new," I added, just to fill the silence.

"Me too. I'm working at the riding stables." He dusted off his jeans, and the faint smell of horses, hay, and old leather rose up. "I'm parched. Got any lemonade?"

I filled a cup with ice and he helped himself to the lemonade.

The door opened, and a bunch of people crowded in, jostling and throwing wet towels onto the counter. A couple of moms shoved their guest cards across the counter. "Could you hurry up?" one of them said. "I'm supposed to meet my husband for lunch and I'm already late."

I picked up the clipboard and scanned the list, looking for her room number. "Mrs. Heffelbloom?"

"It's Heffelblower." She took off her sunglasses to glare at me, like that would speed things up. "How long does it take to check a towel in?"

"I've got it." I crossed her name off the list, returned her card, and tossed the wet towel into the bin.

The girl in the pink bikini tapped her long French-manicured fingernails on the counter. "Could we please, please, *please* get some service here?"

"Just a minute. I'm working as fast as I can."

"Then you are in real trouble, honey," said a woman with crocodile skin. She elbowed Bikini Girl out of the way and dumped a soggy towel onto the counter. "I was here first."

I was ready to cry. Ready to walk out without looking back. Let Aunt B get mad if she wanted. Who needed these spoiled, rude people anyway?

Harrison stepped up to the counter. "Excuse me," he said to the woman, "but the sign says, 'Form One Line.'" He pointed to a small printed sign I had overlooked. She glared at him. Harrison fixed her with his calm blue gaze, his arms folded across his chest.

Finally she said, "For God's sake." But she stepped into line, and after that I got the hang of it. Fifteen minutes later the last person left, the bin was full of wet towels, and my first shift was officially over.

I sank onto the stool. "Thanks."

"You're welcome." Harrison shook his head. "The nerve

of some people. Did you get a load of that girl in pink?"

"Trust a guy to notice the skimpiest bikini on the planet."

"I've seen skimpier. I was talking about her sense of entitlement. Like her agenda was more important than anyone else's. People like that really tick me off."

A picture of Camilla flashed through my mind. "Me too."

Evan blew his whistle and motioned everyone out of the pool. He came inside, nodded to Harrison, and said to me, "You survived."

"Did you think I wouldn't?"

"Balance your cash drawer, then sign out and take those wet towels to the laundry. I'll see you Friday. Don't be late."

He left. I counted the cash in the drawer, hit the "total sales" button on the cash register, and verified the printout. I signed it and put it back in the drawer for whoever had the next shift.

Harrison said, "I'll give you a hand with that bin. It looks heavy."

"I can manage."

"Ah," he said. "You're the independent type. At least let me hold the door for you."

He held open the service door while I wheeled the bin outside.

"Thanks." I started for the laundry, the bin rattling over the bumpy path.

"No problem." Harrison slowed his step to keep pace

with mine. In the distance golf carts skimmed across the deep green grass. Laughter and music drifted from the pool. A group of kids wielding tennis racquets scurried across the path, heading for the courts.

When we reached the laundry, the attendant counted the towels, signed my count sheet, and stuck it on a spindle sitting on the counter. "Okay, Haley, you're good to go."

Harrison glanced at his watch. "I've got to take a bunch of nine-year-olds on a trail ride. See you later."

He jogged to the stables and I headed for the dining hall. Since Aunt B was busy mixing potions at Back in Thyme, I was stuck at the resort until she could pick me up. I headed inside to grab something to eat. The smell of sizzling burgers wafted through the air, and my stomach rumbled. In the main dining room a few golfers were still sitting at tables draped with white tablecloths. In the smaller staff dining room off the kitchen I spotted Nora sitting with a couple of waitresses and a skinny guy wearing a grease-spattered chef's apron.

"Haley." Nora looked up from the burger she'd been devouring and dabbed at her mouth with a paper napkin. "How did it go?"

"Evan was ticked because I was three seconds late."

"My fault. I shouldn't have kept you this morning." She waved her hand at the two waitresses, who were sitting across from her with their feet propped on vacant chairs. "Annie and Kellie," she said, "meet Haley."

"Hi," the taller of the two said, waving a French fry in my direction. "Want a fry?"

The guy in the chef's apron said, "She doesn't want your cold, soggy ones, Kellie." He turned to me. "What about it? You want some fries? A burger? The grill is still hot."

"That would be great. I'm starved."

With her foot, Nora nudged an empty chair. "Take a load off."

"I'm CJ, by the way," Chef Boy said. "I'm interning this season, practicing on the hired help." He opened the freezer, took out a plastic bag, and headed to the kitchen.

"If we die of poisoning, nobody cares," Annie said.

"Very funny." CJ dumped a clump of frozen fries into a vat of simmering oil. "I haven't noticed you turning my food down."

"It's edible," Annie said, grinning. "Just don't go thinking you're the next Emeril or anything."

Just then Frankie came in, red-faced and puffing. "Will someone please tell me why they had to put the garbage cans at the far end of the universe?" She grabbed a napkin off the table and wiped her face. "At least tomorrow it's somebody else's turn."

She opened the fridge, took out a can of soda, and popped it open. CJ said, "I'm making a burger and fries for Haley. You want some?"

"No, thanks. I have to get home. Mom has her meeting this afternoon, and I'm stuck with babysitting Crystal Marie."

She rolled her eyes in the same way Peyton used to when Mom made him babysit me. I thought about the good times I'd had playing ball or watching TV with my big brother before he turned mute and left me behind.

"I'll bet your little sister likes having you around," I said.

The whole room exploded with laughter, and my face flamed. What was so funny? I was right back in school, standing in front of my locker with the whole class laughing at me. My stomach heaved. I ran outside.

"Haley?" Frankie yelled, but I kept running all the way to the stables, past a couple of glossy brown horses cropping grass, past an old Volkswagen bus that looked as if it had escaped from a hippie museum. I sat on the ground with my back against an old tree and let the tears come. I was never going to fit in anywhere. My life *was* over, and there was no use pretending it was ever going back to normal. I was sick with the knowledge that I was stuck here all summer with no way to face Nora and Frankie and the rest.

I wasn't aware of time passing until I heard a shout and saw Harrison and his kids returning from their ride. They were singing a song about cowboys and horses as Harrison led them into the clearing. I pressed against the tree, hoping he wouldn't see me sitting there puffy-eyed, red-faced, and miserable. He dismounted and began lifting the kids off their horses.

"Hey, Harrison," a boy yelled. "Can we go again tomorrow?"

"I'm off tomorrow, buddy, but we can ride on Friday if you want."

"I have to go home on Friday," the kid said.

"I don't," said a little girl in Heidi braids and a pink shorts set. "We're staying all next week."

"Maybe I'll see you again, then," Harrison said as a dark-green van with the resort logo on the door arrived to pick up the riders. Then he led the horses inside. I stood up and jogged across the meadow, my sneakers swishing through the thick grass. I almost made it back to the paved walkway, but Harrison caught up to me. "Haley? Is that you?"

I pretended I hadn't heard, but he grabbed my wrist, turning me around. "What are you . . . oh, man, you've been crying. What's wrong? Did Evan ream you out about something?"

"I'm all right. Just leave me alone, okay?"

He dropped my wrist. "Sure. If that's what you want."

"What I *want* is a new life!"

"A lot of people do."

"I have to go. My aunt is coming to pick me up."

"Okay. I'm off work tomorrow, but I'll be around if you want to talk or anything. People say I'm a pretty good listener."

"I'm off tomorrow too." I started walking.

"Great. You want to hang out?"

I whirled around. "*Why* are you pestering me? God!"

Hurt flickered in his eyes, making me feel ashamed, but I couldn't take the words back. He wheeled around and strode back to the riding stables. I continued toward the parking lot behind the main building to wait for Aunt B.

A few cars were parked in the employees' spaces at the back. I sat on the steps, concocting excuses to quit my stupid job, but it was hopeless. Aunt B would go right out and find me another one, and I'd have to start all over.

The door opened. A pair of ketchup-stained sneakers appeared at my elbow. Annie said, "Haley? How come you took off like that?"

I shrugged.

She plopped down beside me. "CJ was crushed that you didn't stay and eat his masterpiece."

"I lost my appetite."

She sighed. "People are trying to be nice to you, and you keep kicking them in the teeth. Nora said she and Frankie invited you twice to go out with them and you said no. What's up with that?"

"Maybe I just don't like hanging out, okay? Maybe I think it's a stupid waste of time. Maybe I have better stuff to do."

"In a nowhere town like Copper Springs? I doubt it."

"They laughed at me. *You* laughed at me. For no reason."

"We weren't trying to be mean. Crystal Marie is Frankie's mom's bichon frise. Frankie's mom won't set foot outside the house unless someone is there to look after that six-pound ball of fur, and poor Frankie usually gets stuck with dog duty."

Just then Kellie came out jingling her car keys. "Ready, Annie?"

"Sure." Annie got to her feet.

Kellie glanced at me but spoke only to Annie. "Let's make tracks before Chef Forster sees us. A couple of the waitstaff haven't shown up, and I do not want to pull a double shift. My feet are killing me."

They started for the parking lot. "Bye, Haley," Annie said. "Lighten up, okay? Otherwise it'll be an awfully long summer."

They crossed the parking lot and got into Kellie's car, a dark-blue Chevy with a bunch of stickers plastered onto the back bumper. Kellie gunned the engine and they peeled out of the lot just as Aunt B arrived.

"How did it go?" my aunt asked as I got into the car. "Did you meet some nice girls?"

"Uh-huh."

Aunt B swung the convertible onto the road and put her turn signal on. "You see? I knew this was the right place for you this summer. You're going to have a swell time."

Yeah, I thought. *Swell.*

Chapter Seven

Annie was right about one thing: There wasn't much to do in Copper Springs. The next morning, my day off, I caught a ride with Aunt B and wasted the whole morning poking through a bunch of so-called antique stores filled with odd assortments of glass bottles, old postcards, moth-eaten clothes from the 1950s, and musty-smelling books with broken spines.

I was thumbing through a box of tattered movie magazines when a voice behind me said, "Who buys this junk anyway?"

Harrison, in shorts, sandals, and a dark-green T-shirt that said STRESSED IS DESSERTS SPELLED BACKWARD peered at me through a row of bookshelves. He held up both hands, palms out, like he was warding off blows. "I'm not stalking you, I promise."

He really did have a poster-worthy smile.

"Sorry about yesterday," I said. "I was having a bad day."

"It happens." He fished a couple of pieces of sheet music from a cardboard box and headed for the cashier's booth. "See you at work."

He left, jingling the bell over the door on his way out. I spent another half hour at the jewelry case, looking at rhinestone earrings and rows of bracelets made of bright red plastic, until it was time to meet Aunt B for lunch. As I crossed the street near the amusement-park carousel, Harrison was getting into the green and purple hippie van I'd seen parked in the meadow. He pulled onto the street just as Aunt B came out of Back in Thyme.

"That is some vehicle," she observed. "The last time I rode in one of those, it was 1968 and I was on my way to a war-protest rally in Chicago." She locked the store and put her sunglasses on. "Are you hungry?"

"Not really."

"Haley." Aunt B caught my chin in her hand. "How long before you tell me what's bothering you?"

"I'm okay."

"You haven't been yourself since you got here. Something is wrong."

My throat closed up. "There's no use in talking about it. It can't be fixed."

"Of *course* it can be fixed!" Aunt B's kitten-heeled san-dals slapped against the concrete as she hurried to keep up with me. "The only things we can't do anything about are death and taxes. What is it, honey?" she asked as we stopped at the corner and waited to cross the street. "Boy trouble?"

"I wish it were that simple." And then, without meaning to, I spilled the whole story: the pranks, the name-calling, the e-mail encouraging suicide, and Camilla's band of cannibals feeding off my misery.

We reached the restaurant and took a table on the outdoor patio. After we'd ordered iced tea and Caesar salads, Aunt B said, "What do your parents say about this?"

"They don't know."

"It's just like you to pretend everything is fine so others will be spared. Like the time you and Peyton fell out of the tree house."

I'd turned seven that summer. Peyton was eleven, and my hero. I'd climbed onto the branch that hung above the tree house just to impress him. When I got scared, he tried to rescue me, and we both tumbled to the ground. Peyton got a couple of bumps and bruises and carried on like he was dying. Nobody knew my foot was broken until it swelled and turned blue.

I toyed with the cheese shaker. "What good would it do to tell Mom and Dad when they're thousands of miles away? They'd just worry, and anyway it's over."

The waitress brought our food. Aunt B sifted a generous amount of parmesan onto her salad. "It isn't over. Not when the fallout is making you so miserable." She speared a forkful of salad. "What are you planning to do about it?"

"I'm thinking of transferring to another school next year. Or moving to Siberia."

"You're willing to let those girls win? Willing to give up your work at the paper rather than fight back?"

"You don't understand. I can't fight back."

"Why not?"

"Everybody is against me! I can't take on the whole school by myself."

"Bullying is like a forest fire, Haley. It spreads until somebody turns around and faces it, and does something about it."

"Easy for you to say." I pushed my plate away.

"You think I'm giving advice about something I haven't experienced? My first year as mayor a couple of council members tried to railroad me into selling off half the historic district to a developer who wanted to build a Big Mart right in the middle of downtown." She sipped her tea. "When I refused to consider it, the newspaper ran a nasty editorial, questioning my motives and my loyalty to the town. People I had known for twenty years snubbed me on the street."

"But everyone here loves you!"

"Now they do. Because I would not be pushed into doing something I believed was wrong. Because I was willing to tell that developer to stick his proposal in his ear." She leaned across the table. "At some point you're going to have to stand up for yourself. It's at times like this that we find out what we're made of."

Maybe she was right, but I couldn't even imagine

standing up to Camilla and my former friends.

Aunt B said, "Try not to let this situation spoil the fun you could have here with the kids at the resort."

The waitress refilled our iced tea glasses. "Did you ladies save room for dessert?"

Stressed is desserts spelled backward. Maybe Harrison had a point. I looked at Aunt B. "Apple pie?"

"With vanilla ice cream," my aunt said to the waitress. "Two scoops."

When we left the restaurant, Aunt B said, "Since this is my late night at the store, I can take you home now, or you can spend the afternoon at the country club and I'll pick you up later."

The pool at her club was huge, there was a giant snack-bar, and I wasn't in the mood to sit home alone watching sitcom reruns on TV and worrying about my future.

"I have to go get my swimsuit."

"We'll get you a new one!" Aunt B trilled. "There's a wonderful shop just down the street."

Half an hour later I walked out of Oceans with a baby-blue tankini, a pair of flip-flops, and a bottle of suntan lotion. Aunt B dropped me at the entrance and handed me her member card. "If you get hungry before I get back, just grab something at the snack bar." She waved as I got out of the convertible. "Have fun!"

The pool was crowded. At the far end half a dozen girls in bikinis were lying on towels, reading and soaking up the sun. A couple of lifeguards watched over the diving board and the kiddie pool near the snack bar. Music blared from a kiosk selling magazines, candy bars, and soft drinks. I changed into my swimsuit, bought a magazine and a soda, and settled into a chair. I was halfway through a quiz titled "Is He the One for You?" when a voice said, "Hey, there."

Evan dropped into the chair next to mine. "Whatcha reading?"

I closed the magazine. "Nothing important. What are you doing here?"

"Hanging out, same as you. I love swimming, but when I'm on duty I can't enjoy it." He waved his hand toward the lifeguards. "Here, somebody else is in charge."

He stood up, a bronzed god in tight black trunks. "Let's cool off. You do know how to swim, right?"

"Of course."

"Prove it."

"I don't have to." I opened my magazine to hide my confusion. Was Evan *flirting* with me? Or just being his usual obnoxious self?

He grabbed my hand and pulled me to my feet. We were so close I could smell his suntan lotion. Tiny water droplets clung to his eyelashes. I felt as if a big heat lamp had switched on inside my chest.

"Come on," Evan said, breaking the spell. "Unless you're chicken."

Without waiting for him, I strode to the far end of the pool and dived in, slicing cleanly into the water. I kicked to the surface and glided to the side of the pool.

"Okay," he said, smiling down at me. "You *can* swim.

And by the way, you're pretty when you smile."

I got out of the pool and went back to my chair. He jogged around the pool deck, climbed the diving board, and jackknifed into the deep end, sending water splashing onto the nearby bikini squad. Evan swam to the side of the pool and said something that made them laugh. He gestured with his hands, and they hung on his every word, as if he were imparting the secrets of the universe.

Just then Annie walked up and plopped down beside me. "Haley."

"Hi." I tore my gaze away from Evan the Magnificent and toweled off.

"I saw you flirting with Evan." She pawed through her faded denim bag and took out her sunglasses, suntan lotion, and a well-thumbed copy of *The Great Gatsby*.

"I wasn't flirting. He dared me to prove I could swim, and I took him up on it. He's totally into the bikini babes over there."

"Evan is totally into whatever girl he's with at the moment." Annie slathered lotion over her arms and legs. "He's like every other guy on the planet: programmed at birth to care about nothing but sex, sports, and food."

The brittle edge to her voice made me wonder whether Evan had stomped her heart flat, like Frankie had said, but I really didn't want to know. Even if he hadn't meant a single word he'd said to me, his attention made me feel that maybe I wasn't completely invisible after all. Annie opened her book. I went back to my magazine quiz, but I couldn't stop thinking about what Aunt B had said about standing up for myself and not letting my problems back home ruin the whole summer.

The next day, when Evan invited me to the regular Friday night staff party at the pavilion, I said yes.

Chapter Eight

Aunt B dropped me at the entrance to the pavilion just as the lowering sun turned the water into a sheet of liquid gold. Music blared over the PA system; people milled around, talking and laughing. Annie and Kellie looked up and waved as I got out of the car.

"Have fun!" Aunt B said. "I'll pick you up at ten thirty."

She left, and Evan met me at the gate. "Haley! You made it."

He looked amazing in a white shirt with the sleeves rolled up and a pair of tight jeans, and he was standing close, looking into my eyes so intently that it was impossible to look at him and talk at the same time. I tilted my head and smiled up at him, playing it cool, but I felt myself falling for him, and I was no match for the feelings churning inside me. I might as well have stood in the middle of a hurricane, yelling for the wind to stop.

Evan said, "I'm really glad you came."

"Me too," I finally managed.

"I need to say hi to some people, but save a dance for me, okay?"

He moved off into the crowd just as Nora and Frankie showed up. Frankie was immediately swallowed up by her adoring entourage, but Nora grabbed a couple of soft drinks, popped the tops, and handed me one. "Cheers. I'm surprised to see you here."

"Evan invited me."

"Evan. Of course."

"Why is everybody so negative about him? He's really sweet."

"So is chocolate fudge, but that doesn't mean it's good for you. Come on, let's rescue Frankie."

Holding on to my cold soft-drink can, I followed Nora through the crowd. We found Frankie sitting atop a picnic table, talking to a couple of guys wearing dusty jeans and checked shirts. "Hey," Frankie said, "say hi to Zach and Travis. They're helping Harrison with the riding program this year."

The taller of the two pushed a lock of reddish-brown hair out of his eyes and said, "I'm Zach."

"Haley."

Travis just nodded and went back to reading the label on his root-beer can, studying it as if it were the greatest piece of literature since *The Grapes of Wrath*.

"They don't talk much, but they're cuter than all get-out," Frankie said, as if they couldn't hear. "I kind of like the strong silent type." She winked at Zach and he laughed. Frankie went on. "Haley, I'm so glad you came because . . ." Something something.

The last part of her sentence was totally lost on me, because I'd spotted Evan laughing with one of the bikini girls from the country club. His arm was draped around her shoulder, and she was leaning against him like she'd collapse if he weren't standing there holding her up.

"That's Elaine Fitzgerald," Nora was saying when I tuned back in. "She works in the personnel office. She's one of the popular girls around here. Everybody likes her."

"That's why she's popular," Frankie wisecracked. She drained her soft drink and tossed the can into the trash. Zach and Travis wandered off in the general direction of the food. Frankie said, "Let's grab some pizza and find a place to park ourselves."

We filled our plates, pushed through the pulsing crowd to the dock, and settled down, our food between us. While we ate, they filled me in on the other staffers. Most were from Copper Springs or surrounding towns, people who already knew each other from sports, school, or other jobs. Except for the Texans Melanie and Phoebe, it seemed that Harrison and I were the only outsiders.

"Don't worry, though," Nora said between bites of pepperoni pizza. "Most of the people here are pretty decent.

Mr. Porter can be a pain sometimes, but he won't tolerate bad behavior."

"Last year he fired two guys for short-sheeting one of the waiters' beds, and they weren't even really mad or anything," Frankie said. "He's pretty strict."

Somebody turned the music up as "Crazy Little Thing Called Love" blared over the speaker system.

"Woo-woo!" Phoebe and Melanie jumped onto a table, dancing and singing along, urging the crowd to "be cool" and "relax."

The guys, including the strong silent types from the stables, cheered them on and sang along with the chorus. It felt so normal that I began to think maybe it was possible to have a good time without looking over my shoulder to see who was gossiping about me.

When the song ended, the Texas girls took a bow and went back to their pizza. Frankie said, "Listen, Haley. About the other day. We didn't mean to laugh at you. Everybody but me thinks it's hysterical that I get stuck babysitting a stupid dog. There was no way you could have known. I mean, who names a dog Crystal Marie?" She shook her head. "My mom is completely insane. Anyway, no offense, okay?"

"It wasn't your fault. I had a bad experience last spring and I'm not over it yet."

"What happened?" Nora peered at me through her glasses.

"A bunch of girls turned on me, including my best friends." I pulled a blob of cheese off my pizza and popped it into my mouth. It tasted heavenly, salty and hot. "This girl named Camilla Quinn started it," I began, launching into my story. "She thinks she's the queen of everything."

"Huh," Frankie said when I finished. "People like that? I treat 'em like a fart in a phone booth and hold my breath till the stench goes away."

Nora whooped, and the next thing I knew, I was laughing too a deep, stomach-clenching laugh that left me gasping for breath. Telling Nora and Frankie about the whole ordeal didn't hurt quite as much as I'd thought it would. I told them about Joe Bob Turner, and how in my worst moment I'd wondered if I could do what he had done.

"But you weren't really thinking about hurting yourself, right?" Frankie asked, her blue eyes serious.

"Maybe for a minute. I didn't actually want to die. But I wanted the pain to stop."

Frankie licked pizza sauce off her fingers. "A couple of years ago, three kids at my school killed themselves in one semester. The counselors said the last two were just copycats, kids willing to pay the ultimate price for attention even though they wouldn't be around to witness it. But I think there's a lot more pain in the world than adults think."

"Nobody at my school would ever kill themselves," Nora said, her eyes suddenly full of mischief. "Because going to school there makes suicide redundant."

We laughed again just as Evan walked out to the pier and held out his hand. "Haley? Dance with me."

He helped me to my feet and we walked back down

the pier to the dance floor. Above me the pavilion lights twinkled, and beyond them lay the summer sky, peppered with stars. The floor was crowded, and Evan pulled me close as a slow song curled into the air. "Great song," he murmured.

"Mmm-hmm." I moved with the music, feeling like I was outside my own body and floating above the whole glittery scene, watching Haley the Outcast, Haley the Invisible, dancing with the hottest guy in town. When the song ended, Evan held on to me, his arms tight around my waist. I looked up at him, and it was one of those moments I knew I'd remember for the rest of my life.

Then Elaine the Popular walked up. "There you are, Evan! Feed me—I'm famished."

Evan let go and said, "See you, Haley."

Then a fast song blared through the speakers. Frankie danced with CJ, the chef in training, whirling and clapping in time to the beat. Nora flirted with one of the other lifeguards. Angie and Joss, the tennis twins, were joking around with Zach and Travis. I watched it all through a dreamy fog, thinking only about my dance with Evan.

After a couple more songs Nora found me, and we reclaimed our spot on the pier. A few minutes later Frankie caught up to us, and we sat for a while, listening to the music, watching the lights from passing boats reflected on the dark water.

A car horn sounded in the parking lot. Lights went on; a few people left. Frankie said, "I gotta go. You want to hang out tomorrow?"

"Sure we do," Nora said. "I'll pick up you up, and we'll cruise by and get Haley."

We gathered our empty plates and walked back to the pavilion. Nora and I walked out together. She dug her car keys from her purse. "Pick you up around eleven, okay? We'll grab lunch at the mall."

Nora left, and a few minutes later Harrison's van chugged into the parking lot. He got out and loped toward the entrance.

"Haley. What are you doing out here by yourself?"

"Waiting for my ride."

"I never figured you for the party type."

"Evan invited me."

Harrison made room for himself beside me on the step. "Not very chivalrous of him to invite you and then leave you here alone."

"It wasn't an actual date or anything. Just hanging out with people. You know."

From somewhere behind us came a squeal, and then a splash as somebody hit the water. Harrison stood. "This is so totally not my scene."

"Then why are you here?"

"I promised Zach and Travis a ride, but if they don't show up in five minutes, I am out of here."

Just then Aunt B arrived, and I headed for the parking lot.

"Haley?"

I turned around.

"If you aren't doing anything Sunday afternoon, why don't you come riding with me? Unless a bunch of new kids sign up tomorrow, it won't be crowded. I'll teach you to tack up your horse and everything. It'll be fun."

Maybe it was the way he looked at me, as if he could see past all the walls I had put up, to the real me hiding underneath. Maybe it was the music pouring from the pavilion speakers, filling the air with silver vibrations. Maybe I was just sick of feeling worthless and afraid of my future.

"Sure," I said. "Why not?"

Chapter Nine

Saturday morning, after Aunt B left for Back in Thyme, I ate a bowl of cereal and flipped through the TV channels, but there was nothing on except cartoons and some chubby guy with a gray ponytail and matching beard yelling about the fabulous deals at his used-car lot. I had plenty of time before Nora and Frankie were arriving to pick me up for our mall crawl, so I logged on to Aunt B's computer to check e-mail, hoping for news that Camilla and her cannibals had been permanently banished to a remote island off the coast of Australia.

No such luck, but there was an e-mail from Dad, describing his trips to Shakespeare's house and the Victoria and Albert Museum, and the play he and Mom had seen the night before. And there was news of my globe-trotting sibling. *Caught up with Peyton last weekend as he and his pals were in and out of London on their way to Paris,* Dad wrote. *He says to tell you hello and he hopes you're enjoying your summer.*

The realization that my whole family was together on the other side of the world made me feel more alone than ever. Even though I complained about having to have dinner with the parents almost every night, being dragged to church at midnight on Christmas Eve, and all the other stuff parents subject teenagers to, deep down I secretly cherished our corny traditions. What if something happened and they never made it back?

I was so homesick that I wanted to take the next plane to England, but I hit the reply button and told Dad about my job at the resort, about hanging out at the country club, about the party I'd been to the night before. Through the open window I heard tires crunching on the driveway. Nora tooted the horn. I hit send, grabbed my stuff, and jogged out to Nora's car.

Frankie was in the front seat with Nora, so I climbed into the back, which was littered with CDs, a pair of flip-flops, a crinkled Burger Hut bag that still smelled faintly of pickles and grease, and a tattered copy of *The Orange Girl*. I shoved it all aside, searching for the seat belt. Frankie turned around and studied me over the top of her sunglasses. "Cute shirt."

"Thanks." It was sleeveless, sort of a blue-green color. I wore it with a pair of faded-denim cropped jeans and the flat sandals with turquoise beading that Mom had brought home from Morocco a couple of years back.

Nora drove slowly through downtown Copper Springs, inching past the Saturday morning tourists jaywalking to Sam's Breakfast Buffet and lining up to buy tickets for the amusement park. At the resort exit, a long line of mostly SUVs crammed with tired-looking adults, sun-browned kids, and assorted vacation gear waited to turn onto the main road.

"There they go." Frankie sighed. "And just think, we get a whole new crop of the little darlings this afternoon."

"Don't remind me," Nora said. "Day before yesterday those Miller twins from Minneapolis hit me with a water pistol just as I was carrying a load of dishes to the kitchen. I nearly dropped the whole stack."

"That's what they were hoping for," Frankie said, adjusting the air-conditioning vent. "Little monsters."

"You must get a lot of kids at the pool, Haley," Nora said.

"Yeah, but they aren't too bad, as long as I don't run out of ice cream."

"Just wait," Nora said, accelerating past a logging truck, "until the Wellses get here. They're the worst kids on Planet Earth, and dear old Mom lets them do whatever they want."

Frankie said, "They come here every year, the week of July Fourth. We hate them."

We reached the mall. Nora wheeled into a parking space and we headed inside.

"Where to first?" Frankie asked.

"I don't care," Nora said. "I need another pair of sneakers, and I promised Annie I'd pick up some more of that polish she likes from Nailed Down."

"Let's go there first, then," Frankie said. "You're supposed to buy shoes late in the day, after your feet have had a chance to swell."

We walked past a kitchen store with a display of copper pots in the window, past a candle and soap shop and a mattress store, and rode the escalator to the second level. After Nora bought Annie's nail polish, Frankie wanted to check out some earrings that were displayed in the window of an exotic-looking store called African Treasures.

The saleslady explained that the jewelry was made by a group of women in a small village in Ethiopia, and that many of them didn't have any other way of earning money to feed their children. I wasn't sure if the story was true or just a sales pitch designed to separate rich Americans from their money, but in case the saleslady was on the up and up, I bought a pair of earrings made of blue glass beads, and a wooden bracelet with giraffes and elephants carved into it. Nora bought a leopard-print scarf and a pair of sandals, ignoring Frankie's advice about swollen feet.

Frankie picked out some huge wooden discs with shiny black beads decorating the edges and held them up to her ears. "How do they look?"

Nora cocked her head. "Should we make something up or do you want the truth?"

Frankie said, "Over the top?"

"Totally."

"I'll take them," Frankie told the saleslady.

By then we were starving and headed for the food court for chicken nuggets, fries, and sodas.

As we dug into the food, Frankie squeezed a blob of ketchup onto her plate and said, "So. Haley. How was your dance with Evan last night?"

"Awesome. But I'm sure he just felt sorry for me, being new and younger than you guys."

"Evan?" Nora shook her head. "Evan doesn't feel sorry for anybody." She pointed her plastic straw at me. "Don't get mixed up with him, Haley."

Frankie said, "He broke her heart last summer and she still isn't over it."

"I am, too."

"Are not." Frankie downed a couple of chicken nuggets and wiped her fingers on a paper napkin, then looked at me. "Nora's right. Summer romances are bad news. They never work out. It's better to find some cool guy in your high school."

"High school is lame," I said. "The boys are totally lame. There is nobody there to be interested in."

Nora took a long pull on her straw. "Maybe some great new guy will show up. You never know."

"Hey," Frankie said. "You aren't crying, are you?"

I scrubbed at my cheeks and took a drink of soda to loosen the hard knot in my throat.

"You can't let those girls get away with ruining your life forever," Frankie went on.

"You don't know what it's like," I said.

And Frankie, who had just taken a huge mouthful of

soda, sprayed it all over the table. She grabbed a handful of napkins out of the metal holder and blotted it up. "Sorry. That was gross. But Haley, open your eyes. I am a fat girl. Fat! Do you know what it feels like to walk into a room full of fake, spoiled blondes and have them actually move away, like my size is a contagious disease?"

Nora said, "Nobody has a perfect life. In sixth grade, when I went to foster care, everyone laughed at me. Like it was my fault my mother totally messed up."

"What happened?"

Nora rattled the ice in her cup. "She left me and my little sisters in the car at the mall while she went in to pick up a dress she'd had altered. We waited for her for *hours*. Finally I took the girls inside and we looked everywhere for her. Turned out she had run into an old friend—"

"An old *boyfriend*," Frankie amended.

"Yeah, and Mom totally forgot we were waiting for her. How can a mother forget three kids?" Nora shook her head as if she still couldn't believe it. "Anyway, she and this guy had gone clubbing, and the cops called child protective services, and we went to foster care while the authorities investigated my mom for child neglect. It was in all the papers. Everybody at my school knew. It was awful."

She shrugged and smiled, but not before I saw the pain in her eyes. I wadded my greasy napkin and finished the last of my soda. "Did they put her in jail or anything?"

"Nope. She had to go to parenting classes and we had to have official supervision for a year. But it's cool now." Nora stood, shaking off her sadness. "I think my feet are as swollen as they're going to get. Let's hit the shoe store."

We bought sneakers, saw a movie at the multiplex, then headed for home. When we passed the sign for Copper Falls, Frankie said, "Nora! Let's go climb the cliffs. We haven't been up there since they reopened the trail."

"No can do. It's getting late. And besides, that place gives me the creeps."

"Because that kid fell last spring? It was his fault; he ignored the signs warning him to stay on the trail." Frankie poked Nora's arm. "Come on!" She turned around. "You're up for it, right Haley?"

"It sounds dangerous."

Frankie laughed. "Of course it's dangerous! That's why we're doing it."

But Nora said, "I don't have time. Mom is working late tonight and—"

"You have to babysit."

Frankie grinned and Nora grinned back, two friends so totally in synch with each other that they finished each other's sentences. My throat went tight again.

"Haley?"

I realized Nora had asked a question I'd missed. "Sorry. What?"

"Have you signed up for movie night yet?" She turned right at a stop sign covered with graffiti.

"Not yet."

Nora stopped in front of Frankie's house, a white Colonial with dark-green shutters and neat flower beds framing both sides of a brick walkway. Frankie unfastened her seat belt. "Don't wait too long. All the best costumes will go early, and you'll wind up having to dress as a giant primate for the annual screening of *Planet of the Apes*."

As Frankie gathered her purse and her African Treasures shopping bag, Nora held up one finger. "Major idea! Let's meet at the office tomorrow and sign up together."

"Already signed up," Frankie said. "But you two go ahead."

"I can't. I promised Harrison I'd go on a trail ride tomorrow."

Frankie said to Nora, "Get a load of her. First she's dancing with the head lifeguard, and now she's going riding with the resident poet. Or songwriter. Or whatever they say he is."

"It's no big deal," I said.

Frankie grinned. "Whatever. I gotta go. See you."

She ran up the walk. I got out of the backseat and into the front with Nora. The seat was still warm from where Frankie had sat, and the air smelled faintly of her perfume.

Nora glanced at her side mirror and pulled back onto the street. I said, "Harrison is a songwriter?"

"That's the scoop. Hard to tell for sure. He keeps to himself a lot. You know Kellie? From the dining hall? She says he has the people skills of chicken pox, but she's just mad because she wanted to hang with him at the staff party and he was all, 'I'm not even going there.'"

"He seems nice. He helped me out at the pool house on my first day."

"Weird, though," Nora said, "that he lives by himself in that hideous van rather than in the staff housing. Not that I blame him; I hear the cabins are grim."

We got to Pinecrest Drive and sped up the hill to Aunt B's house. Nora said, "They say he's only seventeen but he's emancipated."

"You mean like a freed slave or something?"

She laughed. "When minors can't stand their parents, they petition a judge to allow them to be on their own. If the judge agrees, then their parents can't tell them what to do. A lot of teen movie stars do it so they can take control of their earnings. I read about it in a magazine."

It was every teenager's secret fantasy: unlimited money and no parents anywhere in sight. I got out of the car and retrieved my bag from the trashed backseat. Nora pushed her sunglasses to the top of her head. "Listen, Frankie's right about the costume thing. You should sign up as soon as you can."

"I will."

She left, tooting the horn at the bottom of the driveway, and I went inside. Aunt B was sitting at the dining-room table with poster board and Magic Markers. "There you are. Did you have a good time?"

"Uh-huh." I dropped my stuff onto the table. "We saw the new Marci Harwell movie."

Aunt B looked up from her careful lettering job, a streak of green marker on her chin, her fingers smudged with half a dozen different colors. "Was it any good?"

"It was okay. Car crashes, girls in bikinis, lots of blood. The guys in the theater loved it."

"Of course they did! Those Hollywood people have forgotten there are intelligent people in the world who like movies that actually say something."

She finished coloring in a huge exclamation point and leaned back in her chair to consider her masterpiece. "There! That should get their attention."

I read over her shoulder. JUST SAY NO TO PROP TWO!

"What's Prop Two?"

"The stupidest idea the city council has ever put on the ballot, that's what." Aunt B capped her markers and placed them into their clear plastic case. "They want to take out all the free parking along Pine Avenue and put in parking meters. It will absolutely kill the businesses downtown. People will drive clear out to the mall just to save a dollar on parking fees. The downtown merchants are planning a protest during the Fourth of July weekend."

She picked up the sign by the edges and leaned it against the wall. "Are you hungry?"

"Starving. We had chicken nuggets at the mall."

"Come on. I made lasagna and a blueberry cobbler. We'll eat on the porch."

I helped her set the table with pink napkins, matching place mats, and white plates with pink flowers around the edges. Aunt B put on some music, an old recording by Nina Simone, the singer Mom listened to when she took her bubble baths after exhausting days explaining

Keats and Wordsworth to a room full of bored twenty-year-olds.

While we ate, I told Aunt B about the e-mail from Dad, and about my day at the mall with Frankie and Nora. I showed her the things I'd bought at African Treasures.

"I may wear the bracelet tomorrow, when I go riding with Harrison after work," I said.

"Who is this boy?" She plunged her spoon into her cobbler, and the blueberries oozed out, warm and fragrant.

"Harrison Gray. He looks after the horses and takes guests on trail rides."

"He must be new. Last year, Rusty Griffin's nephew was in charge of the stables."

"He is new," I said. But I decided not to tell her that he was the one driving the strange van around town, much less that he was emancipated.

"I suppose it's all right. I'm sure they checked him out before they turned him loose with the guests' children."

"Great!"

"But take your cell phone and keep it on, so I can reach you if I need to. I'll meet you in the parking lot at four thirty sharp."

Later that night I lay in the dark thinking about Nora and Frankie. Their stories *had* made me feel less alone, even though, unlike me, they were hurt by situations they couldn't control. Still, I thought that maybe each person has only so much shame or disappointment inside them. And maybe I had used mine up.

Chapter Ten

Evan was in the pool house when I arrived for my shift.

"Hi," I said, hoping he couldn't see that the memory of our slow dance and the sight of him in his tight white trunks and form-fitting T-shirt had sent my heart stumbling around inside my chest.

"Haley." He finished stocking the freezer and closed the lid. "Give me a hand with these boxes, okay?"

I helped him flatten the empty ice-cream delivery cartons and we stacked them on the concrete porch out back. He glanced at his watch and frowned.

"What's the matter?"

"Too much to get done. Jamie was supposed to restock the freezer after her shift, only she didn't, and then Mr. Porter told me I have to get some stuff written for the resort newsletter by this afternoon." He ran his hand through his hair. "As if keeping a hundred kids from drowning isn't enough."

"I could help," I said, not even caring that I sounded like an overeager kid, trying to impress. "I write for the paper at my school."

"No kidding. Could you handle the pool news?"

"Piece of cake."

"That would be great, Haley. You're the best."

I followed him back inside, my insides doing the happy dance at the thought that Evan actually needed me. He handed me a pen and a yellow legal pad. "I'm supposed to remind people about the safety rules and the hours of operation of the pool."

"That's easy; I'll copy that stuff off the information board outside. What else?"

Evan ran through his list: swim lessons in the kiddie pool on Monday and Thursday, a Hawaiian-style pool party on Saturday night with everyone invited to wear costumes, a reminder to check the lost and found for missing items.

At nine sharp he left to open the gate, and a horde of swimmers rushed in. I hurried through my towel count, set out my clipboard and pen, and checked the ice dispenser. Between selling ice cream and handing out towels, I wrote the pool news and gave each announcement its own title. For the reminders about rules and regulations I wrote DON'T MAKE WAVES. I titled the piece about the kiddie swim lessons TIME FOR TADPOLES. I had almost forgotten how much I loved writing up the news, how much of myself I'd lose if I transferred to a different school.

Evan came in just as I was finishing, and read over my shoulder. "Hey, you weren't kidding. You're really good at this. Thanks for helping me out."

He hugged me, and it made me so shaky that I started to babble. "It's called the inverted pyramid technique. You put the most important information first and the other details in order of descending importance."

"Huh." He helped himself to a cola. Outside, Byron, the other lifeguard, blew a long blast on his whistle.

"That's in case you have to cut the story short." *Shut up, Haley,* said my inner voice. But evidently my mouth had become disconnected from my brain. "Then none of the important stuff gets left out."

"Huh." Evan drained his cup and tossed it into the trash can. "I've got a great idea. Let's catch a movie tonight. Get away from here for a while."

I stared at him, dumfounded. He was three years older than me, cuter than anything, and the most popular boy at the resort. Why would he want to go out with a loser like me? Then my rational self kicked in, and I said, "You don't have to pay me back for writing the newsletter. It was no big deal."

"Is that what you think? That I'm paying off a debt?"

"Aren't you? I thought you were dating that girl who came with you to the pavilion Friday night."

"Elaine? We've known each other since we were babies. She's a friend. We aren't serious or anything." He took hold of both my wrists, and my pulse jumped against his fingers. "I'll pick you up—we'll catch a movie in Pinehurst and grab some pizza. It'll be fun."

Then half a dozen kids rushed in from the pool, laughing and shoving each other in an effort to be first at the ice-cream counter. One of them, a pink-faced girl in a bright orange bikini, checked out the freezer, then said, "Are there any more double-fudge pops?"

"What you see is what you get," Evan told her. "The truck will deliver more ice cream tomorrow." He turned back to me. "So, how about it?"

My mouth went so dry I was sure he could hear my tongue clicking in my mouth as I said, "Sure. Why not? My aunt's house is the yellow one at the top of Pinecrest."

Evan nodded. "See you at seven." He headed back to the pool.

I was still reeling when the time came to meet Harrison at the stables for our trail ride. I slipped into the restroom at the pool, shucked out of my shorts, and slid into my favorite pair of jeans. I raked my hair back with my fingers and hurried down the path to the stables.

By the time I got there, two boys and a little girl were waiting. Harrison was trying to get the kids to make friends with their mounts by handing the horses apples and lumps of sugar. The boys were getting the hang of it, but the girl was near tears.

"He'll *bite* me!" she cried when Harrison tried to help her feed her horse.

"No, she won't." Harrison looked up and nodded to

me as I neared the corral. "In the first place this is a girl horse, and she's very gentle. See?" He held out an apple on his open palm, and the mare grabbed it. He handed the girl another apple. "You try."

He picked her up, one strong tanned arm around her middle, and guided her hand toward the mare, who promptly munched the apple, then lowered her head to be stroked. "See?" Harrison said patiently, his voice gentle and low. "You and old Cinnamon here will be good friends in no time. I can just tell."

The little boys strapped on their safety helmets and climbed into their saddles.

"Hurry *up*, you big baby!" one of them yelled to the little girl. "You're wasting time. Harrison, let's gooooooo!"

Harrison turned around. "Just a minute. Avery's almost ready." He turned back to the girl. "Aren't you, Avery?"

Her lip trembled. "I guess so."

"Good girl. Up you go!" He lifted her into the saddle and handed her the reins. "Hang on a sec while I get Haley's horse ready. Everybody, this is Haley, my assistant cowpoke. Say hi."

"Hi," the boys chorused.

"Hello," Avery said, her eyes still wide with fear.

I patted the horse. "Is this your first time to ride?"

She bobbed her head. A fat tear spilled down her cheek.

"It's practically my first time too, and I'm scared, to tell you the truth. Maybe we could help each other."

"How?"

"Let's ride side by side. Things aren't quite as scary if you have a friend beside you."

Avery nodded. "Mom took her best friend with her when she went to the beauty salon. Mom was afraid to get her hair cut off. But it came out really cute!"

"Well, there you go," I said as Harrison led my horse, a black and white spotted one, into the corral.

He handed me the reins. "Ready, Haley?"

Maybe I wanted to impress Harrison, maybe I wanted to show Avery there was nothing to fear, but for whatever reason I remembered my riding lessons from that long-ago summer camp and managed to land in the saddle on the first try. The little boys cheered. "Finally!" one of them said. "Can we go now?"

"Let's go!" Harrison swung into his saddle. "Hold the reins loosely so you don't hurt the horses' mouths. Keep your heels pointed down, and follow me."

"Are we going up the mountain?" the other boy asked.

"Not today, buddy," Harrison said over his shoulder. "Maybe when you have more experience. Today we'll stay on the flat trail."

We followed Harrison through the gate and into the meadow. The two boys rode side by side behind Harrison; Avery and I brought up the rear. After a few minutes Avery forgot her fear and chattered about the squirrels we saw chasing each other up a tree. Bees hovering in a clump of purple flowers reminded her of the time she'd gotten stung and had to go to the emergency room because she was allergic. I told her I was allergic to the stuff in

Aunt B's shop, and after that we were friends for life.

We rode for half an hour, passing through stands of rustling trees, then skirting a burbling creek shaded by ancient oaks. A resort van was parked nearby. Two staffers were busy unloading a picnic basket and a cooler and placing them on a wooden table beneath the trees. One of the guys waved as we rode up.

"Small group today, Harrison," he said.

"Sundays are usually light. I've got twenty-seven signed up for tomorrow."

He slid to the ground and turned to help Avery down, but she said, "No, thank you. I can do it by myself."

Harrison winked at me over her head. "No kidding."

"Yep. Watch."

Avery wouldn't have won the prize for Most Graceful Dismount, but she didn't fall, either, and she ran to join the boys at the picnic table.

While the kids ate their snacks, Harrison and I walked down to the creek. He picked up a stone and skipped it across the water. "I'm glad you came today. You were a big help with Avery."

"She just needed encouragement to try something new."

He nodded. We listened to the water rushing over the rocks, and the voices of the staffers and the kids at the picnic table. Harrison was so quiet I started to wonder why he'd even invited me to come along if he was going to ignore me, and even more to the point why I'd said yes. Obviously we had less than zero in common.

"Well," I said finally, just to fill up the silence. "Nice day, huh?"

"Don't do that."

"What?"

"Force the conversation. It'll come when it's ready."

He sat down cross-legged on the damp ground and I followed suit. "That's very Zen," I said.

"Ommm," he replied, closing his eyes.

I laughed, and that broke the ice. Harrison opened his eyes and said, "So. Did you have fun at the pavilion?"

"It was fun. Mostly I hung out with Nora and Frankie."

"They seem like nice girls. But I haven't seen all that much of them. I spend most of my time with the horses."

"So we've noticed."

"Oh? Are you keeping tabs on me?"

I felt myself blushing. "Of course not. It's just that you never eat with the staff, and Nora says you don't sleep in the staff cabins, either."

"My van is much more comfortable, and I can practice my guitar without disturbing anyone."

"Oh, right! Frankie said you're a songwriter."

"I mess around with it some. I'm working on a couple of things. Mostly I play other people's stuff. I'm in a band back home in Seattle, but we split up for the summer to earn some money." He skipped another stone. "Frankie says you're a writer too."

"Now who's keeping tabs?"

He laughed. "Touché. What do you write about?"

I told him about the contest at the *Review*. "If I get the byline, I can write about stuff that really matters."

I tried skipping a stone but it sank with a loud thunk. "Does your band play in one town, or go on the road?"

"Right now we play local gigs. There's this guy who runs an alternative radio station in Seattle. He lets us play live once in a while."

"Wow, so I could tune in and hear you sing?"

"Not unless you were standing right next door to the station. It doesn't have much of a broadcast signal."

"But still. I've never known anyone who performs on the air."

A couple of jays settled into the tree behind us and began squawking. Harrison leaned back and closed his eyes again. I watched the sunlight play across his face, waiting for the conversation to return. Finally, without moving or opening his eyes, he said, "That day in the meadow. You said you wanted a new life. What's wrong with the one you've got?"

I told him as much of my story as I could handle. "I'm worried about what will happen when summer's over and I have to face everybody again," I finished. I made my voice matter-of-fact, like I was reciting a grocery list, but tears welled in my eyes. I blinked them away and focused on the feuding jays.

"See, that's why I left high school," Harrison said. "It was total crap. I couldn't stand it."

"You quit?"

"I finished my diploma by taking classes online. I've been accepted to college. If I decide to go."

This is how small my world was: Nobody I knew was considering not going to college. It was just something you did, like brushing your teeth. "And your parents are okay with that?"

"I'm emancipated. I make my own decisions." He sat up. "Don't get me wrong. I care what my parents think. But I have to make my own mistakes. I can't live my life by somebody else's rules."

Just then the van's horn beeped.

"Time to start back." Harrison stood and helped me to my feet. As I rose, a breeze lifted my hair, and Harrison brushed a strand off my face. "Don't let those idiots at your school make the rules for your life, Haley."

We returned to the picnic area, and Avery rushed over to meet us.

"HaleyguesswhatIfound!" she said, as if it were a single word.

"I can't guess."

She handed me a couple of wilting violets. "I picked them for you."

"They're beautiful, Avery. Thank you."

Harrison whistled for the boys. "Okay, cowpokes, let's mount up. It's a long way back to the ranch."

As we neared the corral, I could see the van waiting to take the kids back to their cabins, and higher up the hillside the waitstaff setting up the tables for dinner on the outside patio.

Harrison helped the kids dismount and collected their helmets.

"Bye, Haley!" Avery waved as the van started up the road.

I waved to her and handed Harrison the reins. "Thanks for the ride."

"Anytime. I still owe you a lesson in tacking. I was running late today and had to get it done before you got here."

"No problem." I checked my watch. Five minutes to Aunt B; two and a half hours until Evan.

Chapter Eleven

"I don't know about this, Haley. I doubt your parents would approve."

Well, of course they wouldn't, but I figured there should be some perks to being exiled all summer. And I would die if I had to cancel my first real date with Evan because Aunt B thought I was a baby.

We were in the kitchen, putting away the groceries we'd bought on the way home. I put a couple of jars of spaghetti sauce in the pantry and made room in the freezer for a carton of chocolate mocha ice cream. "I'm allowed dates," I said. "I went out with Jason almost all of freshman year."

She snorted. "And what a prize he was! But at least he was younger than Evan."

"Not that much younger."

She peered at me over a sack bulging with stalks of broccoli and two loaves of foil-wrapped French bread. "I'd feel better if we got your mother's okay before I turn you loose with a strange boy."

"There isn't time! He'll be here in an hour! And he isn't strange. His great-grandfather helped build the resort. Evan has been here practically forever. Everybody knows him."

Aunt B dropped the broccoli into the veggie bin and took her time folding the empty paper sack.

"Besides," I went on, "you're the one who told me not to let Camilla and them ruin my whole summer, and now that I have a chance to go out and have fun, you won't let me!"

Aunt B filled the tea kettle, set it on the stove, and took her favorite mug from the cabinet. "All right. But you are to be home by eleven, Haley. Not one minute later."

"Great! Thank you!" I hugged her and ran up to my room.

I really missed Suzanne and Vanessa then. Half the fun of going out is the anticipation of it, obsessing over what to wear, and now I had nobody to share it with. I couldn't call Nora or Frankie; they'd just tell me I was making a huge mistake.

I chose a gauzy white skirt, a black short sleeved top, and black sandals. I smoothed on some lip gloss, poked my head into Aunt B's office to say bye, and went down-stairs to wait.

By seven ten there was no Evan. I was certain I'd been

had, the butt of some sick joke. I imagined Evan laughing about me with his friends, and self-loathing welled up inside me. What an idiot I'd been to think he would look twice at someone like me. When he finally showed at seven twenty, I was so relieved he hadn't stood me up, and so blown away by the fact he had actually asked me out, that I didn't even ask why he was late. "You look good," he said. "Let's go."

As soon as we got in the car, Evan said, "We can't make the movie now. By the time we get there, it'll be half over. But I've got a plan B."

He punched the buttons on the radio, looking for some music, and finally stopped when a hip-hop song came on. We headed into town.

"Plan B?" I said.

He slowed for a car turning left off the road. "You know Byron, the other lifeguard?"

"I've seen him around."

"He's having a party. I thought we'd stop by."

"I don't know, Evan. I told my aunt we were going to the movies."

"We won't stay long. We'll just say hi to some people, grab some food. I'll still have you home by curfew."

When I didn't say anything, he frowned. "What's the problem?"

How could I explain that I didn't like lying to Aunt B without sounding like a little kid afraid to grow up and take charge of her own life? "Sure," I said. "The party sounds like fun."

"Great." He turned the music up.

On the ride to Byron's we discovered that we both liked literature and history, preferred mustard to mayo, Coke to Pepsi. We laughed at the same things, and we even had the same favorite color: fire-engine red.

"Scariest movie you ever saw," Evan said as we turned onto a wide boulevard.

"*Texas Chainsaw Massacre*," I said, "Or *Silence of the Lambs*."

Evan laughed. "They're both creepy."

"Most boring movie?" I asked.

He thought for a moment. "*Ishtar?*"

"Or *Lawrence of Arabia*."

Then at the exact same time we both said, "I hate desert movies."

It was incredible how totally in synch we were. I felt like a host of angels was hovering above my head, belting out the "Hallelujah" chorus, because I had found the Perfect Guy.

Evan pulled up to a house roughly the size of the Smithsonian. "Here we are."

The wide circular driveway was packed with SUVs and sports cars. A Land Rover and a rusty Volvo were parked on the lawn. Evan squeezed into a parking space on the street between a Jeep and a black SUV with tinted windows and we started up the walk.

The party was in full swing. Music blared from speakers out by the pool. Groups of people stood on the porch and spilled onto the lawn. As we made our way to the house, Evan stopped to talk to almost everybody. It was amazing the way the crowd parted for us, like we were royalty. Guys slapped Evan on the back, laughing and teasing. The girls looked at me with a mixture of curiosity and envy. I held onto Evan's hand, still unable to believe that the one guy whose attention I wanted most, the hottest guy in town, was with me.

Byron detached himself from a group standing by the front door. He jogged over to us and clapped Evan's shoulder. "Glad you could make it, man."

Evan nodded. "You know Haley. She works at the pool house."

"Sure. How's it going?" Byron glanced at me, then muttered something to Evan, and they both laughed. During his shifts at the pool, Byron always goofed around cracking jokes, but there was something mean beneath his wit. I didn't trust him.

"Listen," Byron said, "I've got to go see some people, but make yourselves at home. There's beer and stuff in the kitchen. I'll catch you later."

The house was packed. People were standing three deep around the big-screen TV, cheering for some baseball game; others were grouped on the stairs, balancing plates of food on their laps, their beverage cans parked nearby. On the couch in the living room a couple was making out, as if they were the only two people on Planet Earth. Music blared from a stereo, competing with the noise of the TV.

Evan said, "I'm going to get a beer. Want one?"

"Just a cola or something."

"Be right back."

He headed for the kitchen just as a familiar voice said, "Haley! What are you doing here?"

"Frankie!"

She grinned and saluted me with her beer can. "I didn't know you knew Byron. But it makes sense you'd have run into him at the pool."

"I don't really know him. I came with Evan."

Her face fell. "Please tell me you're joking."

Somebody turned the music up. The bass pounded through the wall, and I leaned in so Frankie could hear me. "We were supposed to go to the movies, but he was running late."

Frankie took another sip from her can. "What a surprise. Didn't you listen to *anything* Nora and I said about him?"

A couple of guys who waited tables at the resort came in with CJ. One of them yelled, "Hey, Frankie! Wanna hook up later?"

"In your dreams, Jackson."

He made a rude kissing noise and laughed. "Your loss, sweetheart."

"Bite me."

He moved away, laughing with his friends, and Frankie muttered, "Jerk." To me she said, "Listen, I don't want to sound like your mother or anything, but Haley, this crowd is too old for you. *Evan* is too old for you."

Maybe it was true, but I didn't want anybody, even Frankie, telling me what to do. "Evan doesn't think so."

Just then CJ yelled, "Hey, Frankie, c'mere."

"In a minute." She crushed her empty can and said to me, "It's your funeral."

A girl in tight white jeans and a green suede tank top came over and said, "Frankie! Hi!"

"Hey, Alyssa." Frankie gave her a peck on the cheek. "How are things in the gift shop this season?"

"Same old same old. Some kid broke one of those glass figurines Mrs. Weston insists on displaying on the counter. It took me half an hour to sweep up the glass, and then Mrs. W yelled at me for keeping another customer waiting. Like I could do two things at once."

Frankie said, "This is Haley Patterson. She works in the pool house."

Alyssa's eyes widened. "With Evan?"

"Yeah. He brought me to the party tonight."

"Lucky you!"

Evan returned with my soda, said hi to Frankie and Alyssa, then grabbed my hand and led me outside. A fast song started up, and Evan set his beer can on the porch railing. "Come on, Haley, dance with me."

We joined several other couples dancing on the lawn. Evan was laughing, moving closer and closer to me as the music quickened, and before I knew what was happening, he drew me into the shadows and kissed me.

It was the moment every girl dreams about, that first deep kiss with the one and only guy you really want. I could feel Evan's hand at my waist. I put my hands on his shoulders, closed my eyes and kissed him back.

The song ended, and a bunch of guys raced across the

lawn brandishing their beer bottles. One of them crashed into me, and beer sloshed all over my top and dribbled into the waistband of my skirt.

"Omigod! My aunt will *kill* me if she smells beer on my clothes!"

Evan ran inside to get paper towels. I blotted my shirt, but it was soaked through, all the way to my skin. I looked around for Frankie. Maybe she'd switch clothes with me, even if they wouldn't fit very well. But I couldn't find her.

Evan said, "There has to be a laundry room in the house. We'll throw your stuff in the wash. Nobody will ever know."

"It's dry-clean only," I said. "And there's no time. If I miss curfew, I'll be grounded for life."

Evan ran his fingers through his hair. "Gosh, Haley. What are you going to do?"

"Let's go," I said. "Maybe it'll dry before we get home."

In the car Evan turned the AC on full blast, and I held my soggy shirt away from my skin, hoping to speed the drying process. He fiddled with the stereo the whole way, hardly speaking to me at all. When we got to Aunt B's, the living room was dark, but the lights were on in the kitchen. "Great," I muttered. "She's still up."

"Listen," Evan said. "In spite of everything, I had a really good time."

I fumbled for the seat belt and punched the orange release button until it finally disengaged. "Whatever."

"Hey," he said, "you're not mad at *me*, are you? It wasn't *my* fault that jerk ran into you."

No, but it was your fault for showing up late, making me miss the movie, taking me to a beer bust. I smiled. The same old never-make-waves Haley. "I'm not mad at you, Evan."

"That's a relief." He unfastened his seat belt and put his arm around me. "Because I really, really like you. I couldn't stand seeing you at work and being afraid to talk to you. You're my special girl, right?"

The very words I'd dreamed of hearing, but I was too worried to savor them. "I have to go."

"One second." He took a fine-tipped marker from the glove box and started drawing on the back of my hand.

"What are you doing?"

"Shhh. Close your eyes."

I closed my eyes. The tip of the pen pressed into the skin on the back of my hand. "Evan—"

I opened my eyes as the porch light came on. "I have to go."

His lips brushed mine. "Okay. See you tomorrow."

He left, and I went inside. Aunt B was in the kitchen rattling spoons. The microwave beeped.

"Haley?" she called, as if she were expecting somebody else.

I headed for the stairs. "It's me. G'night!"

I hurried up the stairs, but not fast enough. She came into the foyer. "Wait a minute!"

I turned around, my heart pounding, hoping she couldn't smell my shirt, which was still damp and sticky. I clutched my bag to my chest.

"How was the movie?"

"Okay." I faked a yawn. "I'm really tired, though. And I have work tomorrow."

"I'm making hot cocoa," she said. "Want to keep me company?"

"No, thanks. I'm full. Too much soda."

The microwave beeped again, and she turned back to the kitchen. "All right. See you in the morning."

I ran up to my room, switched on the light, and looked at the back of my hand. *UR #1*. I stripped off the shirt and my soggy bra and buried them in the darkest corner of my closet, then stood in the warm shower with my arm sticking outside the curtain so I wouldn't wash the ink off. The whole night replayed itself inside my head like a great movie: the music, the excitement of that first warm-all-over kiss in the dark, the way being with Evan made me feel worthy again. The fact that of all the girls in Copper Springs, I was #1.

Chapter Twelve

I was standing in front of the mirror the next morning, agonizing over my hair, wanting it to look perfect for the moment I would see Evan, when Vanessa called.

"Haley? Listen, I know you're mad at me, not that I blame you, but don't hang up, okay?"

I missed her so much that tears sprang to my eyes. I stared out my window at the green curtain of pine trees in the distance.

"Are you there?" Vanessa asked.

"I'm here."

"So, how are you? How's it going?"

"Like you care."

"I do care." She sighed, and I could imagine her running her fingers through her hair the way she always did when she was agitated. "I miss you, Haley."

When I didn't say anything, she went on. "Amy called. There's news from Ridgeview."

"Camilla and Suzanne fell off a cliff?"

"Something better."

Downstairs the front door opened, and Aunt Bitsy strode to the curb to pick up the morning paper. She was wearing the same yellow caftan she'd worn the day I arrived, and the wind billowed the sleeves, making her look like a goldfinch poised for flight.

Vanessa said, "Amy said that Camilla has spent the last few weeks making life miserable for Angie Gill, a new girl from Chicago who has been hanging out at the Ridgeview pool. Apparently this Angie girl was getting way too popular with the guys, and Camilla started harassing her, calling her names, jamming her locker at the pool house."

"With Suzanne's help, no doubt."

"Who knows? If it means anything, Haley, I haven't spoken to Suzanne since you left."

"Too little too late." My throat closed up.

"I'm trying to make up for it now, if you'll just listen."

"Fine. I'm listening."

"Last week, Camilla started a nasty rumor about Angie, just like she did about you. Angie called her on it, and they got into a shoving match. Camilla knocked Angie down, and she hit her head on the edge of the pool and had to go to the hospital. So now Angie's parents are filing charges against Camilla."

"So what? Her dad will pay the hospital bill and Camilla will get away with it. She always does."

"Maybe not," Vanessa said. "Remember Hannah Bontrager?"

Hannah. My stomach clenched. I remembered her walking into homeroom on the first day of freshman year wearing a long gray dress, heavy black shoes, and a sheer white bonnet covering her hair. It had taken Camilla all of two hours to start a whispering campaign, calling Hannah a "Jesus freak," folding her hands in mock prayer every time Hannah walked past. Hannah hadn't fought back. Like me she'd walked around confused and wounded, her big dark eyes silently pleading for someone to help.

The day before homecoming a bunch of us were standing on the stairs near the *Review* office, waiting until the auditorium opened for the pep rally, when Hannah edged her way through the crush of people pressed together on the stairs, murmuring "sorry" and "excuse me" as she made her way down.

Later, after Hannah was taken to the hospital with a cracked rib and a bruised shoulder, Camilla claimed Hannah had tripped over her own feet, but I know what I saw: Camilla's suede-booted foot darting out to trip Hannah, sending her tumbling down the stairs. Except for Vanessa and Suzanne, I hadn't told anyone.

Hannah transferred to another school, and I told myself it wasn't my fault, that I wasn't a part of it. But I hadn't done anything to stop it either. Maybe it was true that what goes around in life comes around. Maybe I deserved everything that had happened to me.

"Haley?" Vanessa said. "Are you still there?"

"Yeah."

"So anyway, Hannah's family heard about what happened to Angie, and they are coming forward to tell the authorities what Camilla did to her."

"What does this have to do with me?"

Vanessa sighed. "Do I have to draw you a picture? If you tell them what Camilla did to you, it would prove that she's a bona fide bully. Who knows? She might even have to do time in juvie." Her laugh came over the phone. "Can you imagine Camilla trying to style her hair and keep her manicure fresh while being detained in a *correctional* facility?"

Just then Aunt B knocked on my door and stuck her head in. "It's almost nine."

I held up one finger and she closed the door.

"Listen, Vanessa, I have to go."

"Okay. But are you going to tell?"

I thought about how hard it would be to tell Mom and Dad about the condom episode and the suicide e-mail. I tried to picture myself walking into a courtroom, swearing to tell the truth, pointing out Camilla to a blank-faced judge. It would be a huge relief to start sophomore year without having to look over my shoulder every minute. But if I failed, if nobody believed me, life would be a thousand times worse. "I don't know."

"Think about it," Vanessa said. "The case comes up in September."

"I'm late for work."

"Okay. Listen, can I call you again sometime?"

Oh, yes. Please, yes. I miss you so much. "I guess so."

We hung up. I jogged to the kitchen, scooped up a bagel, and met Aunt B in the car.

"All set?" she asked as I slid into my seat.

I nodded and bit into the bagel.

"So, did you have fun with Evan last night?"

"Yeah."

"What movie did you see?"

"*The Scorpion.* With Marci Harwell."

"I thought you saw that movie last week with those two girls who took you shopping."

Busted. "Um. I did, but Evan hadn't seen it, so I watched it again."

The explanation seemed to satisfy her. She changed stations on the radio, and guitar music came on. I made a mental note to take my shirt to the dry cleaner as soon as possible.

Fifteen minutes later we pulled into the parking lot at the resort. I got out of the car, waved, and headed for the pool house. Byron was out back, flattening a couple of delivery cartons.

"Hey," he said. "How's it going?"

"Good. Where's Evan?"

"Called in sick, but don't worry. It isn't fatal. I'm covering for him this morning and he's taking my shift this afternoon."

I counted the towels, readied the cash register, and checked the ice machine. Byron grabbed a set of keys and a bottle of sunblock. "Look, I'm sorry about last night. Those guys shouldn't have been horsing around like that. Did you get into trouble?"

"No, it's cool." I checked the message Evan had inked onto the back of my hand. Parts of it had faded, and now it looked more like hieroglyphics than a status statement. Still, it made me happy to look at it.

Byron went outside to unlock the gate. A couple of older ladies wearing straw sun visors and flowered swimsuits came in for towels, followed by a noisy crowd of middle schoolers wanting sodas and ice cream. A toddler fell and skinned his knee, and his mom came in for a Band-Aid and a popsicle. It was all a big blur. I couldn't stop thinking about my conversation with Vanessa. When I imagined sitting down with Mom and Dad, telling them everything, having them judge me, I froze.

"Haley?"

Byron came in with a yellow legal pad and a stack of papers. "Um. Evan said you're good at writing stuff. There's another newsletter due at the end of the week, and he said you'd help me out."

I perched on the stool behind the cash register, glad for the distraction. I jotted down a story about the tadpole swim meet Evan had organized, a recap of the winners of the hula contest at the regular Saturday night luau, a reminder of the safety rules, and an announcement of a new schedule for the upcoming Fourth of July celebration.

Just before the end of my shift a bunch of people came

in to check in their damp towels. Two girls in matching green bikinis came in for ice cream and sodas, and the kid with the skinned knee came back for another Popsicle. By the time I finished with everything, it was after two o'clock, and I was starving.

I verified the cash-register receipt and the towel count and left the newsletter copy in Byron's wire basket. I opened the door to wheel the wet towels to the laundry, and there stood Harrison in his usual jeans and boots, with a purple and white T-shirt featuring a picture of an open-mouthed trout and the words BORN TO FISH.

He grinned and lifted one hand in a lazy salute.

"Hi," I said, surprised at how happy I was to see him. I indicated his shirt. "Were you?"

"Were I what?"

"Born to fish."

He laughed. "No way. My band played at a catfish festival last summer, and this shirt was what I got instead of a paycheck."

He held the door and I wheeled the towel cart outside. He fell into step beside me. "Are you hungry?"

"Starving."

"Me too. I was thinking about hiking up to the falls for a picnic. The view from there is amazing."

We reached the laundry. "What about your trail rides?"

"The next one isn't until four thirty. There's plenty of time, if we leave now."

"I don't know, Harrison. I need to sign up for movie

night." *And be sure Evan is okay.* I handed my towel cart over to the attendant and waited while he verified the count and signed my slip. Harrison and I walked back outside.

Harrison said, "You can sign up later; the office is open till six. I've got sandwiches and chips. If you don't mind tuna."

He looked so hopeful I couldn't turn him down. "I don't mind."

"Great. Let's go."

I followed him down the trail and waited in the shade while he got our lunch from the van. We set off along a narrow, overgrown path that led upward from the trail. Soon we were climbing through stands of trees that shimmered green and gold in the breeze. I followed him up the steep hillside until we reached a clearing and stopped to catch our breath.

Harrison handed me a bottle of water, opened the other one, and took a long sip. "Almost there. Wait till you see."

"I'm glad you know the way," I said when we started walking again. "A person could get lost up here."

"It's pretty well hidden, but the view is worth it." Harrison indicated an outcropping of gray rocks jutting above our heads. "Be careful up there. The trail is narrow. It can be dangerous if you're not watching where you're going."

"Did someone die up here?"

"That's what I heard. Some kid wandered onto the outcropping and lost his balance."

As we neared the falls, the air grew heavy with the scent of pine. The dull roar of rushing water filled my ears. Harrison held my hand as we inched our way to the top. The vegetation thinned to almost nothing, and I could see a glistening column of water spilling into a dark pool far below.

"Wow." I wiped my brow. "It's beautiful."

"Yeah."

We sat on a flat rock and unwrapped our sandwiches. Waiting for my breathing to slow, I sipped my water and tipped my face to the sky, watching the sunlight turn the falls to diamonds.

Harrison munched his chips and washed them down. "How was the party at Byron's?"

Somehow, even though Harrison and I didn't have anything going on, talking about my date with Evan made me feel uncomfortable.

"It was okay," I said. "How did you know about it?"

"This resort is a beehive of gossip. You'd be surprised at how much I know."

I pulled a bit of crust off my sandwich. "For instance?"

"You went with Evan. Frankie was there. Somebody spilled beer all over you. You cut out early."

"I had an early curfew."

He munched more chips. "Was your dream date with Evan as wonderful as you imagined?"

It was just like Harrison to ask the kinds of questions I'd rather not think about. I glanced at the back of my hand. I'd sweated so much on the walk up that the last of Evan's declaration was now just a gray smear across my skin, but that didn't mean the sentiment wasn't real. "Yes," I said. "It was fantastic."

He crushed his empty chip bag and pulled a stub of a pencil and a palm-sized spiral notebook from his back jeans pocket. He scribbled for a moment, closed his eyes like he was trying to memorize something important, then wrote some more.

"Working on a song lyric?" I was dying to know what he'd written, but I understood his need to keep his words private. At the paper I didn't like anyone reading my stuff until it was finished.

"Just some ideas." He put away his pencil and notebook. "Have you ever heard of Charlie Parker?"

"Afraid not."

"I love his music. He said music is about your own experiences, and you have to really live it before it'll come out right. I try to pay attention to what's going on around me, to feel everything. Even when it hurts." He stopped, like he was suddenly embarrassed, and got to his feet. "We should start back."

I drank the rest of my water, and we started down the trail. Harrison pointed out the small things I would never have noticed: different kinds of trees, a fat scorpion sunning itself on a gray rock, a patch of moss that carpeted the rocks like green velvet. I tried to appreciate it, to take it all in, but my brain was on overload, thinking about Evan, absorbing Vanessa's news about the superdiva, and worrying about the beer-stained shirt hidden at the back of my closet.

"Thanks for the hike," I said when we reached the corral where the horses stood munching grass. "It's gorgeous up there."

"Yeah. It is." He stared at me for so long, I started to twitch.

"What?"

"Nothing. I'll see you later."

I hurried up the path to the office.

"Hi," Phoebe from Texas drawled, looking up from her computer screen. "What can I do for you?"

"I'm Haley Patterson. I need to sign up for movie night."

"Sure." She tapped the keyboard and a new screen popped up. "It looks like all we have left is *The Wizard of Oz* on the twenty-fifth. How do you feel about the Cowardly Lion?"

"Is that my only option?"

"Pretty much." Phoebe fingered her necklace, a gold seashell on a glittering chain, while she studied the screen. "There are a couple of flying-monkey costumes left, but trust me, they are way too hot. I've got the Tin Man, but I don't think it will fit you."

"Fine," I said. "I'll be the lion."

She typed my name and employee number into the computer. "There, you're all set. It's lucky you came in when you did."

I looked out the window. Aunt B was just pulling into the lot. "There's my ride. Thanks, Phoebe."

"Anytime. I'll see you on Oz night. I'm signed up to be the Wicked Witch."

I went out to the car.

"How was your day?" Aunt B asked.

"Busy. I hiked to the falls with Harrison Gray."

She backed out of the parking space. "I haven't been up there in a long time. The trail was closed for a while after that tragic accident."

I dug through my bag for my sunglasses. Aunt B said, "Your parents called this afternoon."

"Is everything okay?"

"Fine. They're heading to the Lake District next week. Your mother is excited."

"Yeah, she's nuts about Wordsworth."

"She said to tell you she'll call tomorrow while you're off work so there will be plenty of time to chat."

Talking about Mom reminded me of my conversation with Vanessa and the big mess waiting for me in Ridgeview. I switched the radio on, looking for some music to distract me.

"That boy Evan called."

I thought I'd only imagined a faint expression of disapproval as she said his name, until we got home and I found the shirt I'd worn to the party hanging in my closet, enveloped in plastic from the one-hour cleaner down the street.

I changed into denim cutoffs and a T-shirt and flopped onto my bed to await the Grand Inquisitor, who arrived momentarily and barged into my room without waiting for an invitation.

Deciding to get the whole episode over with as soon as possible, I said, "I'm sorry I lied about going to the movies."

"This kind of behavior is beneath you, Haley," she said in the precise, overly calm voice adults use when they want to scare you.

She made it sound like I'd committed murder. "What about *your* behavior?" I yelled. "You forced me into telling a lie."

"Forced you?"

"You asked what movie I'd seen and acted like you believed me."

"I did believe you! Until I came home at lunch to retrieve some old files from your closet. I opened the door and almost keeled over from the smell." She planted herself between me and the door, like she thought I might try to make a run for it. "You want to tell me where you really went last night?"

"A party at Evan's friend's house. We *were* going to the movies, but Evan got here too late, so we stopped by Byron's instead."

"And you didn't think to call and tell me of your change in plans."

"If I had called and said I was partying at some guy's house, would you have let me stay?"

"Certainly not. You're only fourteen, and I'm responsible for you. And it goes without saying I do not condone your drinking."

"All I had was a soda! A couple of guys were horsing

around, and one of them spilled his beer on me. I admit I lied about going to the movies, but I am not lying about drinking. I didn't take even one sip."

"Fine. Here's the deal. I know better than to forbid you to see that boy, even though it's plain that he's bad news. The harder I try to keep you apart, the more determined you'll be to prove that I can't stop young love. So go ahead and see him at work, at the country club, and at the staff pavilion. But no more car dates. Period."

"But—"

She held up her hand, coplike. "Quit while you're ahead, Haley."

She turned around and walked out.

Chapter Thirteen

Because the Fourth of July fell on Wednesday, Mr. Porter and his staff decided to hold a weeklong celebration, starting on the Sunday before Independence Day and ending with movie night on Saturday. In between were marshmallow roasts, moonlight hikes, and nightly displays of fireworks over Mirror Lake.

The resort was packed, and everyone worked extra hours to keep all the events running smoothly. When I wasn't at the pool house, I was in the kitchen chopping veggies with Frankie and Nora, or helping the kiddie counselors in the crafts room, or hanging out at the stables with Harrison. Travis had quit, saying the kids were too hard on his nerves, so I got a few quick lessons in how to prepare for a ride.

After grooming the horses, I helped Harrison put on

the pads and saddles, being careful to leave a couple of fingers' width between the cinch and the horse's belly. Then the stirrups had to be adjusted before putting on the bridle. Which involved learning a whole new vocabulary. I learned the difference between a martingale and a noseband, and how to use a halter and a headstall. Harrison showed me how to separate the mouthpiece from the reins and hold it to the horse's lips.

On Saturday I helped tack up the horses for the afternoon ride, then hurried back to the pool to help Evan with the water volleyball tournament. In the days since Aunt B had issued her edict, Evan and I had managed to spend a couple of afternoons together at the country club, and on Wednesday night, after the fireworks, we'd gone to a staff party with Frankie and Nora and the usual crowd at the pavilion. Later that night, making out in the deserted pool house, Evan couldn't have been sweeter. He totally understood Aunt B's decision, and he didn't blame her for wanting to protect me. We were stretched out on a lounge chair, facing each other, our noses practically touching, listening to music on the boom box. I wound my arms around his neck and rested my head against his chest. I didn't let myself think about what would happen in the fall. I wanted summer to go on forever, with Evan, the music, and the dance of moonlight on the lake.

Now, as I rounded the pool house, Evan handed me a clipboard and said, "There you are! Could you check in with the next two teams and be sure everyone is here?"

"Sure. No problem."

"Thanks. You're the absolute best." He jogged around the pool deck, grabbed another can of soda from a cooler, and blew his whistle. The game started, and I went inside the pool house. Elaine, the girl I'd seen with Evan that first night at the pavilion, was sitting on a stool, scribbling on a notepad.

She tossed her pen onto the counter and stretched. "What a week, huh? Mr. Porter is *such* a slave driver."

"Yeah, it's been pretty intense."

She took a fudge pop from the freezer. "I'm starved. You want something?"

"That's okay. I'll grab something with Evan later."

She unwrapped her ice cream and took a dainty bite. "Gosh, this tastes good. So, you and Evan, are you together?"

"Pretty much." A rush of pleasure coursed through me. It still seemed so unreal that out of all the girls he could have chosen, Evan had picked me.

Outside, Evan blew two quick blasts on his whistle, and people cheered as the game went on. Elaine finished her ice cream and wiped her fingers on a paper towel. "I should get going. Mr. Porter asked me to make sure all the stuff is ready for the staff reception. He'll have a cow if everything isn't perfect."

"Is that *tonight*?"

"Uh-huh. There was a memo about it in your pay envelope last week."

I remembered reading the memo, but I'd been so busy I'd forgotten about it. Evan and I were planning to watch the fireworks together, and anything that didn't concern him was way off my radar screen.

"It's a command performance," Elaine continued. "The resort owners are here for the holiday, and Mr. Porter wants to impress them with how well he manages his staff. So wear something cute and smile like this is the best job you've had in your whole life."

"It's the only job I've had in my whole life."

She laughed and pushed open the door. "See you."

I called Aunt B to ask her to pick me up as soon as my shift ended. Up in my room, I tried on three different outfits before finally deciding on a peach-colored skirt and top that showed off my tan, and a pair of kitten-heeled sandals.

"What time should I come back?" Aunt B asked as we pulled into the parking lot just before seven.

"I'm not sure. It's movie night and the whole staff is supposed to help out. After that there's fireworks. I'll get a ride with Frankie and Nora."

"If they can't give you a lift, call me. No matter how late it is."

"I will."

"No riding in the car with Evan."

"Okay! I get it!"

I went inside the main building. Round tables covered with white cloths and decorated with vases of red, white, and blue flowers were positioned around the room. In the corner a string quartet tuned their instruments. Annie and Kellie arrived and took up positions near the back door. Annie waved to me, and I waved back. Phoebe came in with CJ, and Nora and Frankie made a beeline for me.

"Haley, you look awesome!" Frankie, dressed in cargo pants, a white shirt, and her African Treasures earrings, took a sip of cola and wiped her lipstick off the rim. "That is totally your color."

"Thanks."

Nora grabbed my hand. "Love the nail polish. Can I borrow it?'

"Sure." I was relaxed, feeling more like the girl I used to be.

Just as the music started, the Buddha arrived with two other men wearing summer slacks, open-necked shirts, and navy blazers.

"They must be the owners of this outfit," Nora said, narrowing her eyes. "Look at how Mr. Porter is falling all over them."

"They sign his paycheck," Frankie said. "What else can he do?"

Annie and Kellie detached themselves from the wall. Annie said, "You guys? You have to taste these little cheese thingies CJ made. They're amazing!"

Kellie rolled her eyes. "She thinks anything CJ does is amazing."

"I do not!" Annie said, blushing. "I happen to think he's a talented chef, that's all."

Nora said, "There's Phoebe. I need to talk to her about my costume for movie night."

"Good luck," Frankie said. "I got practically the last one myself."

"I'm already signed up to be Princess Leia when we screen *Star Wars*. But the costume came back from the dry cleaner without the headpiece. Phoebe was supposed to call them to see if they have it. Princess Leia just won't be the same without those weird twirly braids."

She left. Frankie studied the people milling around the refreshment tables. "You know who's not here? That guy from the stables."

"Harrison never shows up for stuff like this," I said. "Crowd scenes are not his thing."

"He'd better hope Mr. Porter doesn't notice he's missing." She pushed her hair out of her eyes. "I'm starving. Let's find food."

"Later. Hey, Frankie? Can you give me a ride home tonight?"

"I came with Nora, but I'm sure it'll be okay." She waved to a couple of girls I didn't know. "Meet us in the parking lot after the fireworks."

She started for the food tables just as Evan arrived. "You look great," he murmured, slipping his arm around my shoulder. "I love your hair that way."

I was still basking in the glow of Evan's compliment when the Buddha and his bosses came over. "How are *you*?" Mr. Porter said, in the fake, overly friendly voice people use when they have no idea who you are and hope you won't notice.

"Fine, thank you," I said.

Mr. Porter clapped Evan on the shoulder and introduced him to the two men. "Jim, Henry, I'd like you to meet Evan Cole, our head lifeguard. He's been with us for three years now."

The two guys nodded to me—Miss Nameless—and shook Evan's hand.

"Evan does an excellent job of managing our aquatics program," the Buddha gushed. "I don't know what I'd do without him."

"Thank you, sir," Evan said. "I enjoy working here."

Mr. Porter nodded. "By the way, Evan, you've done a fine job writing the newsletter this season." He chuckled. "'Time for Tadpoles.' Very clever! Where do you come up with that stuff?"

I waited for Evan to tell Mr. Porter that I was the one who had written every word, but Evan just grinned, and I realized that I couldn't totally trust him.

Mr. Porter and his entourage moved off, and Evan squeezed my hand. "Let's grab some food. I'm starving."

I followed him to a serving table and filled my plate, even though I didn't feel like eating. I thought about *Lord of the Flies*, and how Piggy had let Ralph get away with pushing him around until it was too late. I wondered whether their story would have turned out differently if Piggy had stood up for himself from the beginning. But Piggy kept silent and missed his defining moment, and right then I missed mine. I swallowed my irritation and smiled up at Evan like everything was the same, even though we both knew it wasn't.

As we stood around drinking soda, eating CJ's culinary experiments, and talking with the other staffers, Evan seemed suddenly ill at ease. I could feel him pulling away, putting distance between us, and a cold, sick fear settled in the pit of my stomach.

I tried to shake it off as we left the party and made our way up the paved path to the amphitheater. Tonight's movie was *Yankee Doodle Dandy*, an old biopic starring James Cagney, which someone had obviously chosen for its patriotic title. It was Annie's turn to play dress-up; like several other girls she was wearing a 1940s costume complete with hat, white gloves, open-toed pumps, and hose with dark seams running up the backs of her legs.

"Here." She handed me a stack of programs and pointed me toward one of the entrances, where resort guests carrying lawn chairs, blankets, and picnic coolers waited to find seats on the grassy lawn. "Make yourself useful."

Evan said, "I'm supposed to help run the projection truck. I'll catch you later."

I tipped my face toward his, expecting a quick good-bye kiss, but he lifted one hand in a little half wave and headed for the truck parked at the rear of the amphitheater.

"Haley?" Annie jammed her hat back into place over her springy curls. "Don't forget to smile."

I didn't feel much like smiling, but I plastered on a grin and headed for the nearest entrance, scanning the program as I went. The outside was embossed with the Copper Springs logo in green and gold; inside was a list of the cast members and a synopsis of the movie. *Cagney's*

1942 Oscar-winning turn as George M. Cohan features famous song and dance sequences. Happy Fourth of July from the staff at the Copper Springs Resort.

I helped people find places to sit. I repeated, "Enjoy the movie," about a million times before the crowd finally quieted and a large white light illuminated the rectangular screen at the rear of the amphitheater. The projector hummed and clicked, and a series of black and white images flickered and settled on the screen.

I could appreciate that Mr. Cagney won an Oscar for his portrayal of a famous song and dance man, but I just couldn't get into the story. After the first half hour I left the amphitheater and followed the trail to Mirror Lake, where the fireworks were to be held, but the excitement of sharing the evening with Evan was gone. I was mad at him for taking credit for my work and mad at myself for letting him get away with it. I sat on a fallen log near the lake, listening to the faint music coming from the amphitheater and the raspy croaking of frogs. Then I heard a girl giggling, and a guy said, "Shhh! Someone's out there."

Evan. Through a darkness that was broken only by light from a few houses on the far side of the lake I saw him standing behind Elaine underneath a canopy of trees, both arms wrapped around her waist. She was leaning into him, her head thrown back against his shoulder. It was like taking a punch to the stomach. There was no air to breathe. I felt myself coming apart, a billion little formerly Haley atoms spinning through the dark into nothingness.

I turned away, desperate to get out of there without being seen. But my shoes hit a patch of loose stones, and they tumbled into the water with small plopping sounds. Evan murmured something to Elaine, and then he was beside me, taking my arm, spinning me around. "Haley. What are you doing down here?"

I couldn't look at him. I didn't want to talk about anything. I just wanted the letting go to be over.

"Get away from me, Evan." I scrubbed at the tears running down my face.

"Listen, I'm sorry if this is hurting you. I didn't realize how you felt about me until Elaine said—"

But the last thing I wanted to hear was Elaine's take on my love life. I could imagine the two of them laughing about me, the loser with the impossible crush, the one everyone secretly pitied.

Beams of light bobbed in the darkness, illuminating the trees as people left the theater and headed to the lake for the fireworks. I took off my shoes and ran, not caring which way I was going. I didn't know who I hated more: Nora and Frankie for being right about him, Evan for pretending he cared about me, or myself for being stupid enough to think I could ever matter to anyone, let alone a guy as cute and popular as he was. I rounded the pool house and raced toward the meadow, my legs and arms pumping, my throat raw with tears, until I stumbled over something warm and solid in the grass. It felt like a body, and I screamed.

"Haley?"

Somehow, the sound of Harrison's quiet, calm voice steadied me. I dropped onto the grass beside him. Then the first of the fireworks, a huge chrysanthemum-shaped one, exploded over the lake in a shower of red, white, and blue sparklers that twinkled as they fell and died in the dark. I sniffed and raked my hair out of my eyes. "What are you doing here?"

"Stargazing," he said. "I do it all the time. How come you're not at the lake with Mr. Wonderful?"

"I felt like being by myself," I rasped.

More fireworks exploded above us. Harrison scooted closer to me until our shoulders were touching. My throat closed up, and I willed myself not to start blubbering again.

"It's not like you weren't warned about him," Harrison said.

"Who said this has anything to do with Evan?"

"Anybody can see you're crazy for him, and he isn't worth it."

I was mortified to admit that I'd trailed Evan like a love-starved puppy, but in a strange way I was relieved to realize that deep down I'd been waiting for him to dump me, to prove once again that I was worthless. Sure, he was fun and exciting to be with: a top-notch athlete, an even better dancer. He hadn't exactly treated me like a queen, and yet falling for Evan seemed like something fate had decreed, and I couldn't have stopped it even if I'd wanted to.

"What if nothing in life is a matter of chance?" I asked.

"What?" Harrison stretched out on the grass again, his arms behind his head. More fireworks flared and boomed overhead, accompanied by the strains of the *1812 Overture* blaring over the resort loudspeakers.

"What if every single thing in our lives is already planned, only we aren't smart enough to see it?"

"Now that," Harrison said, "is the question of the ages. Back in the nineteenth century a bunch of guys formed a club and sat around in the evenings trying to figure out whether our wishes and dreams can change the way the world works."

"That's easy. The universe couldn't care less."

"So you're saying the world is immoral?"

"I'm saying it's totally oblivious to how people feel. Take the ocean, for instance. You can love it, but it doesn't love you back. It will suck you under and steal your breath and spit you back onto the hard sand. It doesn't care that its beauty can make you cry, or that the sound of the tide coming in at night is the best lullaby you ever heard."

"Exactly!" Harrison said. "Have you read anything by Chauncey Wright or Charles Peirce?"

"Not on purpose."

He laughed. "I'll lend you my books if you want. Peirce will blow you away. In one sentence he said what I'd been trying to make my dad understand: The downside of having an identity is that it's really hard to change it. Dad didn't get it."

"He wanted you to be a different person."

"Yeah. He couldn't accept me for who I really am. So I

got emancipated. It's better for both of us this way."

"But do you really believe that people can't change?" I ran my fingers through the cool, damp grass. If this guy Peirce was right, did that mean I was stuck with being a loser and a wimp my whole life?

"I don't know. The whole question of human motivation is like a blob of mercury. Hard to pin down."

The night had turned cool, and I shivered in my sleeveless top. Harrison peeled off his cotton sweater and handed it to me. In the parking lot at the top of the hill car engines rumbled to life as people headed for home. It was getting late, but being with Harrison was like being enrolled in Philosophy 101, only without the term paper and final exam, and what I needed most was some way to think about everything that had happened to me, and whether there was any hope for my future.

Harrison stood. "You want to borrow my book?"

"Maybe later. Nora and Frankie are waiting to give me a ride home."

"I'll walk you up to the parking lot."

We headed up the path, Harrison whistling softly and me thinking about how to transform myself into a new and improved Haley.

The parking lot was empty except for a couple of pickup trucks and a rusted-out van. Harrison said, "Looks like your friends forgot about you."

"The story of my life."

"Come on, I'll give you a ride home."

"Thanks, but I'd better call my aunt."

I took out my cell, and when Aunt B picked up on the first ring, I told her I'd gotten separated from Nora and Frankie and needed a ride.

"Not a problem!" she said, in a voice way too cheery for the time of night. "I just got home from the Prop Two rally. I'll be right there."

While we waited for her, I filled Harrison in on the Prop Two protest. Between her political activities, running Back in Thyme, and my extra hours at the resort, we hadn't had much time to discuss it, but Aunt B had told me she was disappointed that so few people seemed to care.

"She says people will care once they have to start paying for parking meters, and when the local businesses go under, but then it'll be too late. She was really bummed that so many of her friends said they believed in political action but didn't do much about it."

"Sometimes people's beliefs don't have much to do with how they act," Harrison said.

Aunt B pulled into the parking lot. I handed Harrison his sweater. "Thanks."

"No problem. Let me know if you want to borrow my book."

I got into the car. Aunt B said, "Who was that?"

"Harrison Gray. The one who runs the riding program."

Her brows went up. "You're spending a lot of time with him these days."

"We're just work friends. You know."

Aunt B wheeled out of the parking lot and shot onto the street. "What a week! We've both been so busy I haven't seen you at all. And the summer is slipping away." The convertible's engine hummed as we headed up Pinecrest. "Let's go shopping tomorrow. The mall will be open until six, and I need some new duds. I have a date."

"You?" I blurted before I realized how unflattering it sounded. Aunt B was still fairly attractive, considering her age.

But she didn't seem offended. "What a hoot! Arlen Hooper asked me to be his date for his class reunion."

"The car guy." The wind was whipping my hair around my face, and I dug through the convertible's console looking for a rubber band.

"That's him."

"He looks like Santa Claus." I twisted my hair into a ponytail and pulled the rubber band into place.

She laughed. "I guess he does. He's a nice man. I've known him forever."

"Is it serious?" I teased, and she blushed.

"Serious? Lord, no. I'm too set in my ways. We're just friends. Like you and Harrison."

The next day we headed for the mall and spent hours trudging from store to store looking for the perfect outfit for the car guy's class reunion. As we rode the escalator up to the second level, Aunt B told me that the theme of the reunion was an old Paul Simon song, "Still Crazy After All These Years."

"It's a two-day event in the city park here in Pinecrest,"

she said. "They're setting up tents and performance stages to make it look like Woodstock."

I shrugged, totally clueless.

"You've never heard of Woodstock, the biggest concert in the history of rock and roll?"

"Nope."

She sighed. "It went on for days. In the rain. Everybody who was anybody was there. It was stinky and crowded and rowdy . . ."

"Sounds lovely," I said.

But Aunt B went all dreamy-eyed. "It was fabulous."

By the time she bought a couple of skirts, some tee tops, a pair of jeans, and a distressed denim jacket with silver studs all over the front, I was exhausted, but Aunt B got her second wind and kept going. She fished a twenty out of her purse and sent me to the food court while she shopped some more. I had a cola and fries and people-watched until she came back carrying even more packages, and then we headed home.

I went upstairs to change, and when I came down, strange sounds were blaring from the CD player in the den, and Aunt B was in the throes of some kind of seizure. Her whole body was wiggling like a worm on a fishing line, and she was throwing her arms up in the air like a doomed swimmer going down for the third time.

"Aunt Bitsy?" I yelled above the weird racket. "Are you okay?"

"Of course I'm okay!" She shimmied over to the CD player and shut it off. "I'm practicing the old dances for the reunion," she said. "That was the Swim. Here, I'll show you."

"That's okay." Why waste time learning some ancient dance I'd never be caught doing in public?

"Come on, they're fun! When I was in high school we danced a new dance almost every week. There was the Monkey, the Mashed Potato . . . oh, and the Watusi. I *loved* the Watusi." She demonstrated a couple of moves which looked pretty much the same as the Swim. "And the Hitchhike." She wiggled her butt some more and jerked her thumbs out like she was asking for a ride on the highway.

I laughed. "Don't let the guys at the looney bin see you. They'll lock you up for sure."

"I guess I am still crazy," she said, grinning.

She turned the CD player back on and I let her show me the moves for the Freddy, the Boogaloo, and the Frug, which Aunt B said was invented because doing the Twist for too long was totally exhausting. With the Frug you just stood still and moved your arms around. Lame.

After the dance lesson she tried on her new clothes, stressing like a teenager on the way to the prom. Nothing seemed right. One skirt was too tight; one was too frumpy; she worried that her distressed jeans and studded denim jacket made her look like she was trying too hard. She twisted this way and that, checking herself out in the big mirror in the hallway. "What do you think, Haley? This looked cute in the store, but now I'm not sure."

"Don't sweat it, Aunt B. Pick something and go with it."

"But I don't want to embarrass Arlen. I want him to be proud of his date."

She chewed on her lower lip, holding up first one tee and then another against the jeans and the skirts, and I glimpsed my future: a whole lifetime of dressing to please guys.

Finally she decided on a pink tee, an old pair of jeans that she said fit better than the new ones, and a paisley shawl left over from her college days. Then she handed me a couple of the shopping bags we'd brought from the mall.

"I know your birthday isn't until the seventeenth, but I couldn't resist. These are for you."

I like new stuff as much as the next girl, but I was almost afraid to look. Suppose the bags were full of broomstick skirts and silver studded jackets? But she had stuck to the basics: cute T-shirts, a short denim skirt like the one I'd worn to my interview with the Buddha, and a gold bracelet set with a tiny ruby, my birthstone.

"Happy early fifteenth birthday!" Aunt B said. "We're going to celebrate all month."

"Thanks, Aunt B." I hugged her and went back to my room, feeling let down despite all the loot.

Normally I couldn't wait for my birthday. My parents always made a huge fuss, and even Peyton suspended his usual tormenting. Turning fifteen meant that I was finally old enough for my driver's permit, something I'd looked forward to forever. But I didn't feel much like celebrating. I just felt empty and alone.

Chapter Fourteen

Because of my age there were rules about how many hours I could work, and after my forced labor during the Independence Day festivities Mr. Porter told me to take a couple of days off to even things out. On Monday, instead of having to face Evan at the pool, I was home alone. Aunt B was down at Back in Thyme giving a demonstration of some of her new products. After that she was giving a Prop Two speech at the country club before heading for the final day of the Woodstock reunion with the car guy.

I sat on the porch watching a summer storm boil up over the mountains. Thunder rattled the windowpanes, and the sky beyond the lake turned from gray to black. Wind ruffled the pages of my book and I lost my place, which was just as well, since all I could think about was

Evan. I felt stupid, used, and humiliated. I remembered what Harrison had said about the whole predestination thing, but if you ask me, the real question of the ages is why an otherwise sane girl invariably falls for the one guy who is the absolute worst for her. Figure that one out and your place in history is assured.

When the first raindrops plopped onto the porch, I went inside, made a sandwich, and flipped through the TV channels: soap operas, judges listening to people argue about damaged cars and injured pets, infomercials for jewelry and computers, a rerun of a 1989 baseball game. A commercial for a soft drink came on, and the girl in it looked so much like Vanessa that I did a double take. It wasn't her, of course, but that got me to missing her. When she didn't answer her cell, I scrolled through the caller list on my phone, looking for her dad's number in New Jersey. The line buzzed and clicked, and then Vanessa's voice came on.

"Hey, this is the Townes' residence. If you don't know what to do, I can't help you." *Beep.*

"It's me. Haley. I was just . . . um, call me later if you—"

"Haley?" Vanessa said. "I can't believe I almost missed you."

She sounded breathless but otherwise normal, as if the hurt and ugliness of last spring were just a bad dream. "I just got out of the shower. Daddy-o is taking me to lunch in the city today. He says he has a surprise for me."

"You don't sound too excited about it." I poured a cup

of leftover coffee and popped it into the microwave.

"Because I'm not. I'm pretty sure he's about to tell me he's marrying Irene. He and Mom haven't been divorced a whole year yet and already he's hooking up with some-body else. It's disgusting."

The microwave beeped. I took the coffee out and got some milk from the fridge.

Vanessa went on. "If that woman calls me 'lamb' one more time, I will barf all over her Jimmy Choos."

"Maybe she'd get the point if you started calling her 'beef.' Or 'pork.'"

Vanessa laughed. "Daddy-o would throttle me. Irene isn't exactly Miss Svelte. But he can't keep his hands off her. Basically he has ignored me all summer. If it weren't for Kit and Josh at camp, this summer would be a total zero."

Kit and Josh. A pang of jealousy went through me, even though it wasn't realistic to expect Vanessa to spend the whole summer without making any friends. I took my cof-fee into the living room, switched on the lamp, and curled up on the sofa.

"So," Vanessa said, "what's up? Met any cool guys?"

I skipped the whole Evan story, which was starting to bore me anyway, and told her instead about my upcom-ing role as the Cowardly Lion for movie night and about the new clothes Aunt B had given me on Sunday, an early birthday present.

"I'm sorry we can't be together for your birthday this year," Vanessa said. "Remember last year?"

How could I not? After pizza and an afternoon of swimming with my friends at the Ridgeview pool, Mom rolled
out a spectacular chocolate cake topped with sparklers,
and Dad led everyone in singing the birthday song, very
loud and completely off-key. Peyton gave me a bunch of
gag gifts, including wax lips, a necklace made of orange
plastic beads, and one of those clay figures that you pour
water on to make it grow hair. From Mom and Dad I got
more serious stuff: books, CDs, a couple of DVDs, and
a white denim jacket I'd been wanting forever. Suzanne
and Vanessa chipped in and gave me a gift certificate for
a visit to a day spa. They stayed over at my house after the
party, and we went out for pancakes the next morning.
But that life was over now.

". . . but anyway, that's what Josh thinks." Vanessa
paused. "Are you listening to me, Haley?"

"Uh-huh."

"So. Have you thought about what I said last time?
About telling what Camilla did to you?"

"I can't. Unless you and Suzanne will back me up."

Like *that* would ever happen. The girls at Ridgeview
went by their own set of internal rules, just like Piggy and
Ralph on the deserted island. "I don't have any proof. I
deleted that e-mail and—"

"Wait a minute. What e-mail?"

"Camilla sent it. She said I should kill myself. She
even picked out the day she thought I should do it." The
memory of it made my eyes burn.

"Omigod, Haley, a *death* threat? This is huge."

"It wasn't a threat, exactly. It was more like a suggestion. But it doesn't matter. I deleted it. It's gone." I sipped my coffee, which was too hot and too bitter. I set the cup on the lamp table.

"No, it isn't. All you need is a certain piece of software and you can get it back."

Rain lashed the windowpanes. The lights flickered. A car turned up the long driveway, its headlights making cones of yellow light in the gloom.

"Listen, Aunt B is back. I should go."

"Fine. Use any excuse to keep from talking about this, but you know what you should do, Haley."

"You should have stood up for me, but you didn't. I don't owe anybody anything."

"Okay, whatever. Catch you later." Vanessa hung up.

The door opened and I called, "Aunt B?"

"Surprise!" My brother was standing in the entry hall, dripping water onto Aunt B's shiny hardwood floor.

"Peyton?" When my shock wore off, I hugged him, happy to see him even though he was usually the bane of my existence. "What are you doing here?"

"What kind of a question is that, after seven whole months?" He grinned and shucked out of his raincoat. "How are you, kiddo?"

"Okay, but—"

"I got to thinking about your birthday and figured since Mom and Dad were gone, I should be here to help you celebrate."

I was stunned. "But what about your trip?"

He hung his coat on the coatrack and pocketed his car keys. "I've seen pretty much everything I wanted to see. Corey and Scott are going to Tibet, but I wanted to get back home and have some downtime before college."

"Have you finally made up your mind?"

"I've narrowed it to UCLA and Cornell. But I've got to make a choice soon."

"You want something to drink or anything? Have you seen Mom and Dad? Does Aunt B know you're here?"

"No, yes, and yes," he said. "Mom and Dad are having a ball. They sent you a ton of presents, but you can't have them till your big day. I called Aunt B when my plane landed this morning, but by the time I picked up a rental car and got to Copper Springs it was raining so hard that I didn't stop at Back in Thyme."

Peyton took off his shoes and stretched out on the sofa. "So, how's your summer going?"

I took the chair by the window and gave him the Cliff Notes version of the past month, editing out the part where I acted like a total idiot about Evan. By the time I finished, Peyton was asleep, his head lolled to one side, his lips parted, a thin stream of saliva trickling out. I left him there recuperating from his international flight and went up to my room. My conversation with Vanessa had left me unsettled. Every time she tried to convince me to come forward about Camilla, the fear and shame came roaring back, pulling me back to that place of misery and darkness.

The right thing isn't always the easiest. Dad had written

that once, in an editorial about raising taxes to build a new elementary school in Ridgeview. Maybe telling my story to support the others Camilla had victimized was the right thing to do. But it felt too hard. And now I had other problems to figure out. Like what to say to Evan when I had to go back to the pool house.

Aunt B came home a little while later, and after making a huge fuss over Peyton she cooked an enormous dinner featuring all of his favorites: pot roast, mashed potatoes, and cherry cobbler with vanilla ice cream. While we ate, Peyton entertained us with stories of his meeting with a holy man in India, an encounter with a spitting camel in Egypt, a close call while climbing in the Alps.

Aunt B smiled at him over her third glass of iced tea. "Our little Peyton has turned into a real man of the world."

"I'd like to think I've matured some," Peyton said, reaching for the last of the cobbler. "I was a brat growing up. Haley was the good kid."

"She's still a good kid." Aunt B picked up the pitcher. "More tea?"

Later, after the rain stopped, Aunt B took us for a drive, pointing out to Peyton everything that had changed since his last visit. She told him about my allergy attack the first day I set foot inside Back in Thyme, and Peyton listened politely, even though I had already filled him in. Peyton said he needed some new swim trunks, and since Oceans was already closed, we drove to the mall, where Peyton bought a pair of loose-fitting Hawaiian-print trunks and a sleeker pair of black ones with white stripes down the sides.

"Haley's off work tomorrow," Aunt B told him as we started home. "You two can spend the whole day at the club, if you like."

"Works for me." Peyton turned the music up and sang along with the radio all the way home.

Next morning: Peyton slept till ten, and by the time we got to the country club it was almost noon and the club was packed. Peyton drove around the block looking for a parking spot, and we finally squeezed into an empty space behind a catering van. We grabbed our stuff from the trunk of Peyton's rental car and hiked to the entrance. In the changing room I shucked out of my shorts and tank top, put on my tankini, and headed for the pool.

Peyton was already jogging around the pool deck in his new black Speedo, which made him look like a character straight out of *Baywatch*. He snagged a couple of chairs, and we settled down with our towels, sunblock, and magazines. Peyton plugged in his iPod, put on his sunglasses, and turned his face to the sun. I opened my book, but the noise and movement going on around me made it hard to get into the story. I finally gave up on improving my mind and watched the people splashing in the pool, knots of girls gossiping in the shade of the kiosk, a couple of preteen boys taking turns dunking each other. Beside me Peyton was sleeping again, snoring softly, his sunglasses slipping down his nose.

I grabbed my water bottle and had just taken a long sip when Annie and Kellie arrived. Kellie stopped at the kiosk, but Annie speedwalked around the pool and dropped onto her knees beside my chair. "Haley!"

She put her hand on my arm and squinted at me. "Are you okay?"

I didn't want her pity. I forced a smile. "Sure I am. Why wouldn't I be?"

"We, I mean, I thought . . . you know . . . because of Evan and everything."

A couple of girls squealed, and the lifeguard blew his whistle. Beside me Peyton's iPod slid off his belly. I grabbed it and settled it onto the chair beside him.

Annie pushed her sunglasses to the top of her head and stared at me. "Oh, wow," she murmured, "he's gorgeous. You *know* him?"

"Sure. I've known him forever."

"Where has he *been* all summer? I haven't seen him around here."

"He's been in Europe, India, you name it. He got in yesterday, to surprise me for my birthday."

I didn't tell her that Peyton was my brother and that without him my birthday would be totally sucky. My heart was bruised, and I thought Evan might be sorry if he thought I was seeing some guy who was every bit as gorgeous as he was.

"Does Evan know?"

I shrugged. "Who cares?"

"Right. Listen, Haley. I need a huge, major favor."

Without waiting for me to say anything, she rushed on. "You know CJ, right? The chef in training?"

"I've seen him a few times."

"Kellie said CJ told Nora and Frankie that he really likes me, only he's too shy to do anything about it, and you know me, I'm the same way, so there's this really good chance the summer will end and we'll go our separate ways, and what if we are, like, absolutely made for each other, only we never find out?"

Annie's eyes were so full of hope that I felt afraid for her. I raked my hair out of my eyes. "I'm the last one you should be asking for advice about guys."

"Oh, I don't know. First Evan, and now . . ." She waved her hand toward Peyton. Who chose that moment to wake up. He settled his sunglasses back into place. "Haley. I'm starving. You want a burger?"

"A burger would be great."

He peered at Annie. "Who's this?"

"Annie. She works at the resort. Annie, Peyton. Peyton, Annie."

"Hi," Annie breathed.

"Hey, how's it going?" Peyton turned to me. "You still like extra mustard and pickles?"

"Absolutely. And get some fries, okay? And Cokes?"

"Okay, back in a few."

He left and Annie said, "He remembers how you like your burgers. How romantic is that?"

"Yeah, he's a thoughtful guy."

Annie watched him get in line at the burger kiosk, then

turned back to me. "So anyway, Haley, you know the big staff party is coming up."

"I'm probably going to skip it," I said.

"But you *have* to come!" Annie said. "I'm trying to get up the nerve to talk to CJ, and I need moral support."

"What about Kellie? You two are pretty tight."

"It's her parents' twentieth anniversary and there's this big party at her grandparents' place. Frankie has to baby-sit that night, and I'm sure Nora will keep her company. That leaves you."

Just then I heard a burst of familiar laughter and looked past Annie's shoulder. Peyton was filling our soft-drink cups from the fountain and talking to Kellie.

"You have to come," Annie said. "Be a pal. Say you will."

Just then Kellie looked up and waved to me. I waved back as Peyton came toward us. "Okay," I said quickly, "I'll come."

"Great!" Annie bounced on the balls of her feet like a six-year-old headed for the circus. "See you later!"

She trotted off, waving to my brother as she passed. Peyton arrived with our food.

I unwrapped my burger. "You met Kellie."

"The blonde? She's cute." He bit into his burger.

"What did she say?"

"Who?"

"Duh. Kellie. The person we were just discussing."

He shrugged and took a long sip of cola. "I dunno. Stuff. Nothing to write home about. Not that I ever did."

"Mom and Dad haven't written either, except for

a few e-mails. It's like they forgot I'm on the planet."

"You won't think that once you see all the presents you're getting. I didn't get half that much stuff when I turned fifteen."

"Guilt presents," I said.

He laughed. "Yeah, maybe. Aren't you going to eat your burger?"

I took a few bites and drank half my soda while he scarfed down both servings of fries. We threw away the trash and stretched out on our chairs again. Peyton opened a car magazine and I headed for the water. It was too crowded to swim laps, but I paddled around until Peyton waved me to the side of the pool. The crowd was thinning; Annie and Kellie had already left. I hoisted myself onto the deck.

"Let's call it a day," Peyton said. "I've had enough sun."

We gathered our stuff and headed for the car, still wearing our bathing suits, T-shirts, and sandals. Peyton was in the middle of a story about how he'd almost lost his wallet to a pickpocket in Italy when I looked up to see Evan and Elaine coming across the parking lot, heading right toward us.

As we turned toward the street where we'd left our car, I latched onto Peyton's arm, looked up into his face, and said, "That is so funny!" just as Evan passed by, so close that his shoulder brushed mine.

Chapter Fifteen

When I headed back to work at the pool house on Friday the thirteenth, I wasn't thinking that the day could bring bad luck. I had too much other stuff to occupy my mind: how to act when I saw Evan, how to get out of my promise to attend the staff party with Annie, whether I could keep up the sick pretense that Peyton was my new boyfriend until my birthday was over and he went home. Plus, I was still replaying my last conversation with Vanessa, lining up all the reasons why telling the truth about Camilla was a really bad idea.

I arrived on time and opened the door, expecting to see Evan, but it was Elaine who was sitting on the stool going over the paperwork, her head bent over the clipboard. She looked up and caught her bottom lip in her teeth. "Haley."

For days I'd been so focused on how I felt about Evan that I hadn't even thought about Elaine's role in the whole thing, but seeing her reminded me of our previous conversation, and my anger flared. "What are you doing here?"

"I came to see you."

I turned away and began my towel count, but I kept losing my place and starting over. Elaine slid off the stool and stood between me and the shelves. "Listen, I know you're hurt and embarrassed, and I want you to know I'm really sorry."

"Right. That's why you played me for a fool with your oh-so-innocent questions about me and Evan and whether we were together. You already knew the answer."

"With Evan no one ever knows for sure."

Outside, the gate creaked as it swung open to admit the swimmers. Byron stood on the pool deck near the deep end while the guests filed in.

"Evan and Byron switched schedules this morning," Elaine said. "I came to talk to you while Evan's gone. To explain everything."

"You don't have to explain. I get it."

"No, I don't think you do. Evan and I have known each other since grade school. Our families are friends. We've dated off and on since eighth grade, and sometimes he still behaves with all the maturity of a thirteen-year-old." She straightened a stack of papers on the counter. "I've lost count of the number of times I've broken up with him and told him to stay out of my life. I know he cheats on me with other girls, but I still can't live without him."

Her eyes filled, and I couldn't help feeling sorry for her. She said, "When I asked if you and Evan were together, it wasn't to trap you or make you feel stupid. I had to know if you were serious about him."

"Yeah," I said, "I was. But it's my fault. People warned me about him, and I didn't listen. I wanted to believe he cared about me. But he made it pretty clear that what we had going on was just a meaningless summer thing."

A couple of grade-school boys came in to buy ice cream. I took their orders, swiped their guest cards, and handed them a stack of napkins. They ran back out to the pool.

Elaine's cell rang. She listened for a minute, said, "Be right there," and hung up. "Listen, Haley, I have to go. Don't be mad at me, okay?"

I shrugged and gnawed on a cuticle.

"If it makes you feel any better, I heard that Harrison Gray is crazy for you."

"We're just friends."

"He's a nice guy." Elaine donned her sunglasses. "See you later."

I finished the towel count, handed a couple of them to a girl wearing a blue tankini almost exactly like mine, and for the rest of the morning I filled orders for ice cream and soda, collected wet towels, and replayed Elaine's words in my head. If Harrison was crazy for me, he hadn't shown it. What if Elaine had made it up just to make me feel better? And even if he did care, I wouldn't blame him for thinking that I liked him only because Evan had dumped me. Nobody wants to think they are second choice.

Then Merrie Matheson, who had the shift after mine, arrived.

"Busy day?" She took a compact from her bag and checked her lip gloss.

"No more than usual. The ice machine is running low."

"Okay." She looked around. "Where's Evan?"

"Switched shifts with Byron." I opened the rear door and pulled out the towel cart.

"Too chicken to face you, huh? I'm not surprised after what he did to you. Stupid jerk."

"It's no big deal."

Merrie grinned. "Easy for you to say, since you've got that hottie Peyton to take his place."

I thought about my brother, about the way he teased me until I thought my head would explode. About his endearing habit of leaving wet towels all over the bathroom floor, about how charming he looked lying around the house all day in a pair of ragged pajama bottoms, scarfing down pizza and watching football until his eyes glazed over.

"Yeah," I said. "He's quite the catch."

I started down the path to the laundry with my towel cart, turned the corner, and nearly ran over Harrison. Usually, the sight of him in his message-of-the-day T-shirt was a real day-brightener, but after Elaine's revelation I wasn't ready to talk to him. I needed time to think.

"Whoa!" He jumped out of the way and put out his hand

to stop my cart. "They ought to put brakes on those things."

"Sorry."

"No harm done." He fell into step beside me. "What did you do with your time off?"

"Slept late, went shopping with my aunt."

When we reached the laundry, he held the door for me and waited while I checked my towels in. "Are you done for the day? Want to grab some lunch?"

I was starved as usual, but I just couldn't be with Harrison right then, and I still had some time to kill before Peyton was supposed to pick me up. "I sort of promised Nora I'd help her with the kiddie crafts this afternoon. She's subbing for someone who's out sick."

"Okay." His blue eyes pierced mine, and I hoped he couldn't tell that I had just made up an excuse to avoid being with him. "Listen, I know about your breakup with Evan. So you don't have to pretend with me."

"I'm not! I already have other plans! Why do guys think they have to come first?"

"Hey, don't take it out on me. I'm not the one who hurt you."

All the fight went out of me then. "Sorry. Don't pay any attention to me. I'm a mess today. Too much on my mind."

We started toward the main building. He said, "Want to know what I did while you were off?"

"Sure."

"Went to Pinehurst and sat in on a jam session at a club they've got over there."

"You got to play! That's great."

"It was. But the best part is that I met a guy who runs a local radio station. He heard my set and invited me to come in and talk to him about performing on his show."

"That's great!" I said again, because it really *was* great, and because I was too preoccupied to think of anything more original.

"Yeah," Harrison said. "So anyway, I'm going over there tomorrow night to talk to him, and there's this film festival going on. There's a movie I think you'd like to see. If you aren't too busy."

He smiled, and I wondered whether Harrison did have a thing for me and I'd been so lost in my Evan fantasy that I hadn't noticed. Or maybe he just felt sorry for me because I got dumped, and he decided to ask me out on a mercy date. Which would be worse than sitting home on a Saturday night watching reruns on TV and playing gin rummy with Aunt B.

"I'll have to ask my aunt."

"Well, sure," Harrison said. "We can stop by the radio station first, then see the movie, grab some dinner, and be home by eleven."

He checked his watch. "I'm going to grab a sandwich. Then I have to take a bunch of ladies on a trail ride, but I'll call you later. Or you can call me. Or whatever."

I took a pen out of my pocket, and we wrote each other's numbers on our palms.

I was hungry too, but since I'd invented the story about helping Nora, I walked over to the crafts building and went inside. A couple of girls were setting up for a kiddie class, laying out construction paper, scissors, and glue.

"It is so totally pathetic," one of them said. "The way she was showing him off at parties and at the pavilion, always finding a way to say, 'I'm with Evan,' like they were practically engaged."

"When everyone with half a brain could see Evan wasn't really interested in her. I mean, he was with Elaine every chance he got. Don't get me wrong, I can understand how she'd be mortified after Evan dumped her. But showing up with a new guy right away and flaunting him at the country club? How sick is that?"

They came out to a storage cabinet in the hallway. I ducked into a storeroom crammed with art supplies and crouched behind the table.

"Annie couldn't believe it either," the second girl said. "I feel sorry for the guy. He's really cute, and it's obvious Haley is just using him to get back at Evan. As if Evan cares."

Then she laughed. *Kellie.*

"So anyway," Kellie said, "I'm thinking I should go after this guy. I mean, Haley is cute, but she's not *that* cute, and besides, she's too young for him. He needs a more mature woman."

"That's you, Kel. Mature."

"Shut up. I wonder if he's really into her or whether he's basically unattached."

"Guys that cute are never unattached."

They laughed again. Then Kellie said, "Okay, Gina, this should be enough stuff to get you through the afternoon."

"Thanks for helping me out," the other girl said.

"It was fun. Better than waiting tables, I assure you."

"Yeah, but at least you get tips."

They left, and I headed for the parking lot to meet Peyton, feeling too miserable to cry. I prayed he'd get there before I saw anybody else I knew, but it was Aunt B who wheeled into the lot five minutes later, the radio blaring.

"Where's Peyton?" I slid into the car and fastened my seat belt.

"Off somewhere doing boy stuff. I hate to say it, but I think he's getting bored."

"There's not much to do here," I said. "Maybe he should just take off, you know? If he doesn't want to be here."

"And miss your birthday?"

"I'm not a kid anymore. I don't need the whole cake and candles thing."

"You're never too old for cake and candles. If I didn't know better, I'd say you were trying to get rid of your brother. Did you two have a fight?"

"No." I watched the scenery sliding past, the dark pine trees melding into a blur as Aunt B sped toward home. "There's no use in making him miserable, that's all."

"I don't think he's miserable. He's going to a concert tomorrow night with a couple of guys he met at the country club. Apparently his favorite band of all time is performing."

She put her blinker on and waited to turn left onto our street. "That leaves you and me, kid. What would you like to do?"

"Harrison asked me to a film festival in Pinehurst tomorrow night. Is it okay?"

Aunt B frowned. "We don't know much about him, do we?"

As we headed up the driveway, I thought about Evan, and how I'd been so sure he was Mr. Perfect, when in reality he was a total jerk. "I'm sure Mr. Porter checked Harrison out before he hired him. We won't be late."

She pulled into the garage and cut the engine. "The last time I let you go to the movies with a boy, it didn't turn out too well."

"No detours this time. I promise."

"If this boy changes the plan even one iota, you are to call me at once. Is that clear?"

"As a bell." I figured I should prepare her in advance for Harrison's mode of transportation. I didn't want her freaking out about the van and embarrassing him, so I mentioned the day we'd seen it downtown and how it had reminded her of her hippie days.

"At least if I have to go out looking for you, you'll be easy to spot." She tossed her purse and keys onto a chair. "Home by eleven, Haley. And I don't want you hanging around with kids who are drinking."

"No problem. I'll call and let him know it's okay."

"In my day it was the guy who did the calling."

I went up to my room, called Harrison, and spent an hour rummaging in my closet for something to wear. Even though going out with him didn't give me butterflies the way dating Evan had, I still wanted to look good for him.

Sometimes Harrison seemed too good to be true. I hoped I wasn't imagining him to be better than he was. I had taken the parts of Evan I liked best—his popularity, good looks, and athleticism—and fashioned him into the perfect boyfriend I so desperately wanted, and look at how *that* had turned out. I didn't want to make the same mistake again.

Chapter Sixteen

"Here we are." Harrison pulled into a parking space behind a nondescript brick building in Pinehurst and cut the engine. "KPQR radio." He glanced at his watch. "We're early. You want to grab an ice cream or something?"

"Sure."

He took my hand to help me out of the van and held on as he locked the door and pocketed the keys. We crossed the parking lot and followed a cobblestone pathway to the town square. Like Copper Springs, Pinehurst was an old town that had tried to recapture its glory days by redoing a bunch of the downtown buildings. New awnings, all in the same shade of cranberry red, shaded the doorways of antique shops, jewelry stores, and boutiques. In the middle of the square was a pineapple-shaped fountain surrounded by huge pots of summer flowers.

"The ice-cream shop is over here," Harrison said. "What flavor do you want?"

"Mocha chocolate chip?"

"Grab a couple of chairs and I'll be right back."

I staked out a table near the fountain and listened to the music coming over the speaker system, an old Beach Boys tune about going joyriding in a T-bird. Which reminded me of Aunt B. She had given Harrison the third degree about where we were going, and whether he was a careful driver, and whether the old van had seat belts. I was mortified, but her questions hadn't fazed Harrison in the least. He was patient and respectful, which automatically earned points with her, and it hadn't hurt that he'd worn nice jeans, polished boots, and a crisp starched shirt instead of his usual tee.

"Here you go." He handed me a waffle cone and a stack of napkins. We ate our ice cream and watched the summer people coming and going in the square.

"So," I said, "are you nervous about seeing the radio guy?"

"Nah. Yes!" He laughed. "Only because I want it so much, you know?"

"Yeah. If I don't get that column at the paper . . ." My voice trailed away.

"I heard you were the brains behind Evan's newsletter." He wiped a blob of raspberry sherbet from his fingers. "I knew from the first day that we had a lot in common."

"But you're a songwriter."

"Mostly."

"I think it would be harder to write songs. All that rhyming stuff."

He laughed, and crumpled his napkin. "We should start back. I don't want to keep the guy waiting."

Ten minutes later we were sitting in the office at the station talking to Rick Matheny, the spiky-haired, tattooed program director, who didn't seem much older than Harrison. He leaned back in his threadbare chair and put his feet up on a desk littered with CDs, broadcast tapes, half-empty coffee cups, and a greasy pizza box. "Harrison. I really dig your sound, man."

"Thanks."

"You got any more songs like the ones you played the other night?"

"A few. I'm working on a new one now."

"Let's hear it."

"It isn't ready yet." For the first time since I'd met him, Harrison actually seemed uncomfortable. "It's . . . I'm . . . not ready."

"Okay. That's cool. As long as you have enough material to fill the time slot every week."

Harrison's eyes lit up. "You're offering me a steady gig?"

Rick grinned. "Until the end of the summer; then we'll see. But don't get too excited. We're a small station. Drive fifty miles and you won't be able to pick us up. Still, we have a loyal local following, and a guy's gotta start somewhere."

Harrison jumped to his feet and stuck out his hand. "Thanks a lot, Rick. I really appreciate this."

Rick waved him back to his seat. "We can't pay much, but we'll run some advertising in the local paper, let folks know when you'll be on. And Terry Parsons over at the club is already talking about having you back. You have a band, right?"

"Shades of Gray. But we broke up for the summer, and now my drummer has quit. His dad is sending him to boarding school. For now I'm going solo."

"Bummer," Rick said. Finally he looked at me. "Some people just don't appreciate a creative spirit. It is truly tragic when that happens."

Harrison said, "When do I start?"

"How about next Saturday night? Six to six thirty."

"Great."

Rick stood. "Send me your list by Wednesday so I can make sure we don't have duplications. And mix it up some. I don't want thirty minutes of Beatles covers. Our listeners like to hear something new from time to time."

"You got it." Harrison was positively beaming. It made me feel good to see him so happy.

We said good-bye to Rick and headed for the film festival. As we neared the theater, Harrison pointed to the marquee. "I thought you'd appreciate this movie."

It was *His Girl Friday*, about a female newspaper reporter. I loved it, and I loved Harrison for picking out something he knew I'd really like. We sat in the darkened theater, sharing a box of warm, salty popcorn, and for a while I could stop pretending that Evan's ditching me hadn't hurt at all. Stop pretending to be crazy in love with my own brother.

When the movie ended, we left the theater, and Harrison said, "Are you hungry?"

After the ice cream and popcorn I wasn't, really, but I said, "A little."

"Let's go." He held my hand as we headed back to the van. We left Pinehurst and turned onto the highway to Copper Springs. Halfway there, Harrison braked and took a sharp left onto a narrow, rutted road that climbed upward through dense stands of pines. Here and there the glassy eyes of a deer or a raccoon appeared in the trees. The dark, the stillness, and the unfamiliar road made me nervous. I glanced at Harrison. *We don't know much about him, do we?*

"This isn't the way home," I said. "Aunt B will be furious if we get lost."

"We aren't lost. This road follows an old Indian trail around the opposite side of the mountain and connects with the one that goes past the stables."

A doe and her fawn stepped into the white glare of the headlights. Harrison stopped, and we waited until they flicked their tails and bounded into the underbrush. Easing the van forward, he said, "We're no more than ten miles from the resort as the crow flies, but the view from this side is really something. I discovered it last spring, before the resort opened. Don't worry. You won't miss your curfew."

After another couple of minutes Harrison pulled into

a wide, paved area. As the van made the turn, the headlights swept over a green sign: SCENIC LOOKOUT. He killed
the engine, and we got out and walked a few feet to the
edge of a steep cliff. A fat, pale moon rose just above the
tops of the pine trees, throwing its light into a shimmering
waterfall far below.

My breath caught. "Wow."

Chapter Seventeen

Harrison rested one hand on my shoulder and pointed into the moonlit distance. "There's the trail where we hiked to the falls, and to your left, down there, are the stables."

Now that my eyes had adjusted to the dark, I could make out the dull gleam of the tin-roofed stables far below. Harrison said, "Look behind you."

I turned around. The face of Eagle Mountain, the tallest peak in Copper Springs, pierced the starlit sky. "Up there is Eagle Point," he said. "The local Indians thought it was a sacred place."

"How do you know all this stuff?"

"When I first came here, I bought a book about the area. There's a lot more here than people realize."

"No kidding. I've been coming to Copper Springs for years, and I've never been up here."

"Well, don't go telling everyone about it. Some developer will want to tear the trees out, level the mountain, and put up condos and a strip mall."

"You sound just like my aunt. She's still fighting about those parking meters downtown."

"Hang on a sec. I'll be right back."

He jogged to the van, opened the rear doors, and came back with a blanket, his guitar, and a cooler. He spread the blanket on the asphalt of the parking lot, set his guitar on it, and opened the cooler. "Mademoiselle, your dinner is served."

So, okay, this definitely was not a mercy date. No guy would go to so much trouble just to make someone feel better about being dumped. Harrison smiled at me, and I smiled back, feeling totally confused.

"Have a seat!" Harrison dropped to his knees and peered into the cooler. "Ham and cheese, or turkey and tomato?"

"Turkey, please."

He handed me the sandwich, a bag of chips, and a napkin.

"Coke or Sprite?"

"Coke."

He popped the top, set the can on the blanket next to me, and unwrapped his sandwich. Below us the moonlit falls glittered and rumbled, an owl hooted, insects sang in the trees. "Nature's own sweet music," Harrison said dreamily. "Man has never been able to improve on it. Though many have tried."

We polished off our sandwiches. Harrison took up his

guitar and began to play random chords and pieces of melody, like a kid practicing piano scales.

He sang a few bars of "Country Roads," and when he sang about the road taking him home, I could hear something sad behind the music. Hurt, maybe, or homesickness.

"Will you go home after the summer ends?" I asked.

"Maybe." He strummed the guitar. "Or maybe I'll get famous singing at good old KPQR and stick around here for a while."

"It must be great to be the boss of your own life and go wherever you want."

"It has its advantages, but if you move around too much, one morning you wake up realizing that you don't really belong anywhere."

"I wouldn't mind moving away from Ridgeview. I have no friends there anymore."

I told him that Vanessa had been hounding me for weeks, urging me to tell the authorities what Camilla had done to me. "Vanessa doesn't understand it's a chance I can't take. If Angie and Hannah lose their cases against Camilla, she'll make my life worse than ever. Anybody who testifies against her will be an outcast. It's how things work in high school."

Harrison took a long swallow of soda. "There was this guy at my school freshman year. Farrell Haynes. All the girls were nuts about him, and he took advantage of it. One night at a party he assaulted a girl from my algebra class. He hurt her pretty bad, but Emily wouldn't tell anyone what happened. Farrell was in the popular group;

she was a nobody and afraid people wouldn't believe her. A couple of months later it happened again with a different girl, only *that* girl went straight to the cops. Farrell got arrested."

"Yeah, but what he did was way worse than what Camilla did to Angie and Hannah. And to me."

"Those two girls got hurt," Harrison said. "That's all the authorities will care about."

I sipped my soda. "The girl who told on Farrell was ostracized, right?"

"Some of the girls talked about her for a while, but mostly people admired her courage. The girls who were her friends before were still her friends, and I guess that's about as much as a person can expect."

He strummed the guitar, giving me time to take in his words. At last he said, "If you move away, you'll have to give up your work at the paper. I can't believe you'd even think of letting them take that away from you. You can't walk away from the paper any more than I can walk away from my music. It's the old identity thing. It's who we are."

"I guess."

"You didn't do anything to be ashamed of, Haley." He peered inside the cooler. "You want another soda?"

"No, I'm good. Play a song for me."

"What do you want to hear?"

"Something totally new. Something nobody else in the entire universe has ever heard."

He strummed his guitar. "I was working on a new piece for the band, but I never finished it. Anyway, it starts out:

'Moving through each day we make the road / Proving unafraid to share the load . . .' Then something something something . . ." He stopped and laughed softly. "That's all I've got so far."

It was the kind of old-fashioned seventies-era rock song Dad listened to on Saturdays when he washed his car, but coming from Harrison it sounded fresh and new. "You have to finish it," I said.

"Except I don't have my band anymore."

"You'll get a new one. Or go solo. It'll be a huge hit."

"Yeah. My first number one."

"It'll go gold."

"Platinum."

"Double platinum."

He laughed and got to his feet. "We should go."

We threw away our trash and took the blanket, the cooler, and Harrison's guitar back to the van. He started the engine and backed onto the road. Ten minutes later we turned onto the main highway toward home.

As we neared the center of town we saw a crowd in the park across from the carousel. Nora and Frankie were sitting on the hood of Nora's car, drinking from giant soda cups. Annie was there with CJ; the girls from the tennis courts were sitting cross-legged on the grass talking to Phoebe.

"Looks like we missed the party," Harrison said. "We can stop for a minute if you want to."

Then I spotted a couple standing beneath the trees. The girl laughed and grabbed the guy's arm. He spun her around, like they were dancing. Kellie. And Peyton.

Chapter Eighteen

Harrison glanced at me. "Are you okay?"

"Yep. Just tired. Let's skip this soiree and head home."

He accelerated past the park, and five minutes later we were sitting in Aunt B's driveway. Harrison was talking about William James, about the nature of the universe and the music of the spheres, but all I could think of was that now everyone would know the truth about Peyton, and I would be right back where I'd started at the beginning of summer: a pathetic loser, the object of everyone's pity or amusement. There was no way I could face anyone ever again.

". . . if you want," Harrison said. "Hello? Earth calling Haley."

"Sorry. I have to go." I reached for the door handle.

"Thanks for the movie and everything. I had a great time."

"You're welcome. So do you want it or not?"

"Want what?"

"The book I promised to lend you," he said with the patience of someone reasoning with a four-year-old. "About the metaphysical thinkers."

The last thing I wanted was a dense tome about some old dead guys; I needed a plan for the next twenty-four hours of my life. But Harrison had already turned around and was digging through a pile of books on the floor behind him.

"Here you go." He pressed the book into my hands.

Conversation stopped as we reached the moment when I had to decide whether to kiss him or not. In the end the kisses I'd shared with Evan hadn't meant anything, but even in my distracted state of mind I realized that Harrison *mattered*, and I was totally unprepared for the situation. Harrison sat perfectly still, one hand draped over the steering wheel, the other searching for mine in the darkness.

I leaned over, aiming for his cheek at the same moment he turned his head and our lips collided. He chuckled. "Okay. So, um, I'll see you later?"

Just then the porch light came on, and Aunt B appeared in the doorway. I got out of the van and closed the door. Harrison turned the van around and beeped the horn as he headed back toward town.

Aunt B waved me inside. Over cups of cocoa I filled her in on the film festival and the visit to the radio station, but I edited out the drive to the lookout and the picnic, since technically it breached her rule of no detours and I wasn't up for a fight. Plus, I needed to figure out how to deal with the next big disaster looming in my life.

I rinsed my cup at the sink, then got ready for bed. I tossed and turned all night, dreading having to face everyone at work. When morning finally came and I told Aunt B I thought I was coming down with something, she took one look at my bleary eyes and sent me back upstairs. I called in sick, and after Aunt B left for Back in Thyme, I tried to distract myself with the book Harrison had lent me, but the principles of pragmatism and Kepler's laws of planetary motion were not at all helpful in figuring out how to get out of the latest mess I'd created. If only I had admitted up front that Peyton was my brother. Now it was too late.

I was so deep in thought that the sound of my cell ringing took a while to penetrate my brain.

"Haley," Frankie said. "Where are you?"

"Home. I'm sick today."

"Right."

A few seconds ticked by. Then I said, "Okay. How bad is it?"

"Not as bad as you think. Kellie is all excited that Peyton is unattached. Annie is afraid you're gonna bail on her and not go to the staff party."

"She got that right."

"Listen," Frankie said, "here's how I see it. That day at the country club when you told Annie you'd known

Peyton forever, that was the truth! And you never actually *said* he was your boyfriend, did you?"

"No, but I knew what she was thinking, and I didn't set her straight."

"Not your problem. All you have to do is laugh about how silly a mix-up it was. If you act confident, everyone will assume Annie misunderstood, and it'll blow over. Don't make a huge mountain out of this. It's not that big a deal."

"On top of everything that happened with Evan, it feels huge."

Frankie snorted. "You can be the winner of the dumpee sweepstakes and feel sorry for yourself, or you can go on with your life."

"Right."

"So, are you coming to work tomorrow or what?"

"I'm off on Tuesdays, and besides, tomorrow is my birthday."

"No kidding! Happy birthday! You'll be here Wednesday, then."

"I don't know. Maybe." I'd have to go back to the pool house sometime. Aunt B would never let me quit, no matter how bad I messed up.

"Wednesday," Frankie said. "Don't make me come and get you."

She hung up.

I went downstairs. Peyton was sitting on the couch with the TV remote, eating a bowl of cereal. He lifted his spoon as I headed for the kitchen. "Hey."

"Hi." I took a cinnamon bun from the freezer and popped it into the microwave. The coffee pot was still half full. I poured half a cup and topped it off with milk, wondering why it had always been so hard to talk to Peyton. Despite family vacations and dinner together most nights, we seemed more like casual friends than blood kin. Not that I could blame him for not wanting to admit we were related.

The microwave beeped, and I took the bun out, set it on a plate, and sat at the kitchen table. In the living room I could hear the morning newscaster interviewing some senator running for reelection, then cutting to the scene of a fire in an abandoned warehouse in Pinehurst.

I unwound the bun, tore off a piece, and popped it into my mouth just as Peyton came in to dump his cereal bowl into the sink. He poured himself a cup of coffee and pulled out the chair opposite mine. "How was the film festival?"

"Good. The movie was about a newspaperwoman."

"Right up your alley."

"Yep." I licked sugar off my fingers. "How was the concert?"

"A huge bust. The band I really wanted to see canceled at the last minute, and they brought in some crummy dance band from the fifties." He gulped his coffee. "I cut out early, came back here, and caught an impromptu party in the park. A lot of your friends were there."

"I wouldn't call them friends, exactly."

"That would be news to them. That girl Annie thinks you hung the moon."

"Excuse me. Are we talking about the same person?"

"Frizzy hair? Glasses?"

"That's her."

"She says you promised to help her with her boy problem."

"I'm the last person who should give advice in that department."

"Annie told me what happened with that Evan creep. It's lucky he wasn't there last night. I'd have punched his lights out."

I stared at my brother, totally dumfounded.

He grinned. "What? You think I'd let some jerk hurt my little sister and walk away?"

"People warned me about him, but I wouldn't listen."

"Big surprise. You always were the kid who had to try out everything for herself. Remember when Mom got that new electric range and told you not to touch the burners?"

I didn't remember the details, but I could recall searing my fingers and having to go to the doctor. Then I remembered something else about that day: Peyton sitting on the edge of my bed, feeding me ice cream and reading *The Velveteen Rabbit* aloud until I fell asleep.

"I'm sorry," I said. "For dragging you into my stupid charade. I didn't mean for it to happen. Annie assumed you were my guy and I—"

"Hey, it's no big deal. I mean, is it your fault Annie started a rumor that's completely untrue?"

"Have you been talking to Frankie?"

"Who?" He tried to appear totally innocent, but I could tell he knew exactly who I meant. "She's right, you know.

Sometimes you just have to bluff your way through."

He helped himself to a bite of my cinnamon roll and told me another of his travel adventures, in which some hotel guy in India refused to return his passport. "I told Rajeev that Dad was a diplomat at the embassy in New Delhi and that there would be a huge international incident if he didn't give me my passport at once."

"What if Rajeev had called your bluff?"

Peyton poured more coffee. "I'd have thought of something else. The point is, I acted like I was right, and it worked. You'd be surprised at how often that's the case."

He took one final pull of his java. "I'm going to hit the shower and head for the country club. You want to come?"

"I called in sick. Can't blow my cover."

"Just be sure you're well by tomorrow. It's your big day."

"Yeah."

"Fifteen," Peyton said. "Your childhood is practically over."

I rinsed our breakfast dishes, remembering the year the Chavez family moved into the house down the street from ours. I was in fifth grade and totally in awe of Elena Chavez, who was the most beautiful fourteen-year-old girl I'd ever seen. I tried to copy her walk, her clothes, her laugh. When Mom asked her to babysit me one weekend, I was in heaven. Elena braided my hair, gave me a pedicure with her blueberry-sparkle polish, and showed me pictures of the dress she was getting for her fifteenth birthday. It was made of pink satin, with short cap sleeves and a train. Elena explained that her fifteenth birthday, her *quinceañera*, meant that she was a young woman, with all the responsibilities and privileges of an adult.

I wasn't nearly ready to be an adult; I made too many mistakes. Still, when Mom and Dad called from London the next morning, I went right into my usual act, pretending I was thrilled with my life and everything in it.

"Did you open your presents yet?" Mom asked, after I'd given her the edited version of my summer so far. "Did Peyton get them there in one piece?"

"Yeah. They're unbelievable, Mom."

I'd received a state-of-the-art laptop computer, a couple of cashmere sweaters, and a necklace with my initial outlined in microscopic diamonds. At breakfast that morning Peyton had shown me how to play DVDs on the laptop, and we'd agreed that so much expensive loot was definitely the result of the guilt the parents were feeling at being overseas on my big day.

Dad came on the line and told me about his visit to the offices of the *Times* of London. "I wish you could have seen it, Haley. Our entire operation would fit inside just one floor of their building. I had lunch with a couple of the editors. We may collaborate on a series of articles next year."

"That's great, Dad."

"Hey, maybe we could set up an exchange between your paper at school and one here. Your readers might like to know what goes on at schools across the pond."

He was so full of plans there was no way I could tell him I wanted to leave Ridgeview High, the paper, everything.

Mom recapped a new play they'd seen and reminded me that they'd be coming home in a couple of weeks. She and Dad sang "Happy birthday, dear Haley" until I started to cry. Then Mom lost it, sniffling about how much she missed me and how she couldn't wait to see me and how she just knew that whatever had gone wrong last spring would be fine once we all got back to Ridgeview.

When we got off the phone, Aunt B showered me with more presents, mainly books and CDs. Peyton handed me a heavy cardboard cylinder, taped shut at both ends. "Sorry I didn't have time to wrap it very well, but it's the thought that counts."

I found the scissors, opened the cylinder, and took out a full-size replica of the front page of the *New York Times* for July 17, 1993, the day I was born.

"Happy birthday, kid," Peyton said.

"I love it!" I hugged him, and my brother hugged back. "I'm going to frame it for my room."

"Good idea," Aunt B said. "Who wants cake?"

After we stuffed ourselves with chocolate cake, Aunt B left for another Prop Two meeting. She had closed the shop in honor of my birthday, and Bill the cat was spending the day in our garage. Since Peyton was allergic, I fed Bill and put out a bowl of water for him before Peyton and I left for the country club.

On the way Peyton told me he still hadn't figured out his future. "You're lucky. You've always known you want to follow Dad into journalism. I have no clue."

"But you're good at everything," I said, as Nora's car sped past us. Nora honked, and Frankie waggled one hand out the window. "The world is your oyster."

He fiddled with the buttons on the dash, adjusting the AC. "Dad thinks I should go into banking or law. But I don't know. On my trip I saw so much poverty and ignorance in the world. I want to do something about it."

"Like what?'

"I'm not sure. Teaching is one option, but Mom advised against it."

"What? She *loves* teaching!"

"Sometimes. She's totally into her visiting professorship. But the run-of-the-mill twenty-year-old slackers are wearing her down. She says they don't really care about learning anything; they just want to get the credits, get out, and get on with their lives."

"Like high school," I said, and Peyton laughed.

"Yeah, like that." He slowed for a logging truck entering the highway.

"Don't worry," I said, "you'll figure it out. You've got four years, and then grad school."

Peyton reached over and tugged my ponytail. I smiled at him.

At the country club we parked in the lot next to a dusty, mustard-colored Jeep plastered with bumper stickers. We went inside, bought sodas, and settled into our chairs. Peyton plugged into his iPod. I opened one of the books Aunt B had given me and enjoyed ten whole minutes of peace before the gossip started from somewhere behind me. "There they are," a voice said. "Still pretending. How sick is that?"

"Maybe they really are into each other," another girl whispered. "Like that actress with the huge lips who sucks face with her brother. Ew."

They laughed and started toward the kiosk. I imagined standing up and hurling a couple of well-placed insults that would have them whimpering in total mortification. *You've lost so much weight since the start of the summer; you must have a tapeworm. Too bad your brain is so small in comparison to your boobs.* But of course I said nothing.

Kellie crossed the pool deck, her hips swaying inside her too-tight white bikini. "Hi, you two, what's up?"

Peyton opened his eyes and grunted.

"It's my birthday," I said. "My brother is helping me celebrate."

She pushed her oversize sunglasses to the top of her head. "So you finally admit it?"

"Admit what?"

"Yeah," Peyton said. "What are you talking about, Kellie? I told you the other night she was my kid sister. It isn't a secret."

"But I thought . . . Annie said . . ."

"Annie jumped to conclusions. That's not my problem, is it?" I sipped my cola. "And if you think you're going to make points with my brother by gossiping about me, you couldn't be more wrong."

Peyton picked up his earphones. "Bye, Kellie. See you around."

Suddenly I felt like celebrating. "I'm going to get an ice cream," I said, when Kellie stalked off. "You want anything?"

"Nah, I'm good."

I got in line at the kiosk. The club was crowded; I spotted several of the resort staff, including Elaine, sunbathing near the lifeguard tower. When it was my turn at the window I ordered an orange sherbet, and I had just taken my first bite when someone grabbed my arm, spinning me around.

"Frankie!"

"Happy birthday."

"Thanks."

"Having a good day?"

"Mostly, yeah. I thought it would be grim without my parents, but my brother and my aunt made up for it." I looked around. "Where's Nora?"

Frankie tightened her grip on my arm. "Okay, you need to come with me now. And you may as well know, resisting is futile."

She propelled me along the pool deck, past the spot where Peyton still lay with a towel draped over his head. She slowed down long enough to snag my bag and my new book before leading me out the gate.

"Wait! What are you doing? I need to tell Peyton—"

"Peyton knows."

Nora appeared and fell into step beside us. "You're being kidnapped."

"*What?*" My sherbet was melting; a sticky orange stream dripped down my arm. I licked the cone.

Nora took it from me and tossed it away. "You need a break from all the nasty stuff with that Camilla person, and more recently the totally stupid gossip about you and your 'new boyfriend,' not to mention all the stress of the BOE."

"The BOE?"

"Betrayal of Evan. Although you could have spared yourself that if you'd listened to us." She sighed. "The good news is, now that you've seen his true colors, it shouldn't be all that hard to forget him."

Since my brain was stuck on stupid again, I couldn't talk, so Nora did. "Plus, it's your birthday. Time for a makeover."

Frankie nodded solemnly. "At the Beauty Emporium."

"I can't afford that place!"

"You can, with all the money you've made this summer, but fortunately that won't be necessary. It's all arranged."

Frankie led me to Nora's car and opened the back door with a flourish. "Hop in."

"Wait. I have to call Aunt B, let her know . . ."

"She knows too," Nora said, starting the car and flipping the radio and the AC to full blast.

"So everyone is in on it but me? When did you set this up?" I asked.

Nora backed out of the parking lot. "Yesterday. When you called in sick, we realized the situation was critical and something had to be done."

"So I called my cousin Julian," Frankie said, turning around in her seat. "He's the artistic director at the BE, and when he learned of your sad plight, he agreed to give you a whole new look, pro bono."

"You don't have to thank us now," Nora said, leaning on the horn as a guy in a bright yellow Corvette cut us off. "When you win the Pulitzer just be sure we get front-row seats for the ceremony."

Their protectiveness brought tears to my eyes and gave me a little more hope. If they were willing to go to so much trouble for me, maybe I still had a future. Somewhere.

Half an hour later I was seated in a small private room at the Beauty Emporium, drowning in a sea of pink. Pink chairs, pink drapes, pink carpet, and Julian himself in a pink shirt, black silk trousers, and loafers worn without socks. His hair was scraped back into a tight wheat-colored ponytail.

He took the rubber band off my ponytail, held it at arm's length, and dropped it into the trash can, disposing of it like it was a dead cockroach. "Those things are murder on your hair," he scolded. "Don't let me catch you wearing one ever again. Now sit still and let me think."

Julian dragged a brush through my hair and held it back with one hand while he stared at my face in the mirror. "My god, I would die for those cheekbones, and here you are, hiding them under this bush of a hairdo. Or should I say a hair-*don't*? What are you *thinking*?"

Frankie and Nora, who were perched side by side on little pink embroidered chairs, grinned at each other like proud parents at a dance recital.

"And those eyes!" Julian went on. "Of course nobody notices them with all this unruly hair just hanging there like a hound's ears. Honey, I've made up my mind—this rat's nest has to go."

"Not all of it. I don't want it cut too short."

Julian sighed. "If you can't trust me, then our relationship has no future at all. Come with me; let's get you shampooed."

He shampooed, conditioned, snipped, and dried my hair into a feathered cut that ended at my chin. He tweezed my brows, mascaraed my lashes, brushed bronzing powder over my cheeks, and finished his creation with two shades of lip color. Then he removed my pink cape and spun me around in the chair. "Ta-daaa!"

"Omigod, Haley, you are a freaking movie star," Nora said. "Forget what I said about the Pulitzer. Now I'm talking the Oscars."

I studied my reflection, but with all the makeup it was like looking at a stranger. A beautiful stranger. I raked my fingers through my hair.

"You'll get used to it," Julian said, loading up a pink bag with hair gel, conditioner, mascara, and lip gloss. "Come back in a week if you don't absolutely love it."

"I know somebody who's gonna love it," Frankie said. "Somebody who writes songs and rides horses."

Nora nodded. "He has a thing for you. Everybody says so."

"Everybody says lots of stuff that isn't true." I turned to Julian. "This is really nice of you. Thank you so much."

"Oh, darling, you are more than welcome. Have a fabulous birthday, and knock that lucky songwriting cowboy dead." Julian planted a kiss on the top of my head, then folded Frankie into a bear hug. "Take care, sugar pie. And come back when you're ready to do something with your hair. You could do with a trim."

He followed us into the marble foyer. "Bye-bye!"

We got into the car. Frankie opened the glove box and handed me a small package wrapped in silver paper. "Happy Birthday from me and Nora."

"But you've already done way too much. I can't believe you went to so much trouble."

"Hey, you're only fifteen once. Besides, this is a practical present."

Inside the box was a tiny vial of purple liquid, wrapped in cotton. I squinted at the print on the label. "Amansa Guapo?"

"Oil to tame bullies," Frankie said. "We ordered it online."

"From one of those voodoo places in Miami," Nora added, pulling onto the street. "We were planning to give it to you at the end of the summer, but then we found out it was your birthday."

"I don't believe in voodoo," I said, "but thanks, you guys. That was really sweet." I watched the scenery flashing past, wishing that bully repellent *would* work. Wishing there were some potion or pill that would erase my bad memories. They could name it Memoroff. One dose and I'd forget every horrible thing that had happened to me.

"It won't hurt to sprinkle a little on that Camilla girl," Frankie said, grinning. "Just in case."

Chapter Nineteen

Peyton left the next day. He planned to hang out for a couple of weeks with some of his high-school friends who had moved to California to attend college. He and Aunt B dropped me at the resort on their way to the airport. Aunt B wheeled into the parking lot, and I got out of the backseat. Peyton rolled his window down, and I stuck my head inside the car to say good-bye.

"You aren't going to bawl or anything are you?" Peyton teased. "Because that would be way more embarrassing than being mistaken for your boyfriend."

"Don't flatter yourself. These are tears of joy over getting my bathroom back."

"I'm the one who should be complaining about the bathroom. What do you *do* in there that takes so long?"

Aunt B said, "It's a woman thing, Peyton. We wouldn't expect you to understand."

Peyton grinned. "It's worth the time. You look great, kid."

Aunt B said, "I hate to break up this meeting of the Mutual Admiration Society, but we need to get a move on. I'll be back to pick you up around four."

"Okay. Bye, Peyton. Thanks for coming for my birthday. And . . . everything. It meant a lot."

"Don't mention it. I'll see you back home."

Aunt B turned around and headed for the road, and I started toward the pool house. That morning I had done a fairly good imitation of Julian's blowout of my new haircut, and I'd used a little bit of the bronzing powder. I'd been wearing mascara since eighth grade, but I left off the eyeliner and the heavy-duty lip gloss. Facing Evan for the first time since he dumped me, I didn't want him to think I'd gotten all glammed up in some pathetic attempt to win him back.

Besides, the songwriting cowboy liked the new me. He was standing in the parking lot with a couple of guys, but when he saw me he waved to them and joined me on the path to the pool house.

"Whoa. What happened?"

"It's the new me."

"You look great. Totally different. Not that you didn't look amazing before! I mean . . . it's just . . . different."

It was so unlike Harrison to act so flustered that I couldn't help thinking maybe the talk I'd heard was true and he did have a thing for me. I didn't know how to feel about it. "Nora and Frankie took me to a salon for my birthday."

"It's your birthday?"

"Yesterday."

"No kidding. Why didn't you tell me?"

"I didn't want you to think I was hinting for a present."

We continued walking toward the pool house, waving to people arriving for their shifts. The tennis twins jogged to the courts; CJ the chef hurried toward the kitchen, tying his apron on as he ran. Phoebe and Elaine headed for the office.

"I wouldn't have thought you were hinting around for a gift," Harrison said. "You're not that type of person. If anything, you're too self-deprecating."

"Thanks for the analysis. Now I can cancel my appointment with my shrink."

"I'm sorry! I didn't mean—"

"Hey, Harrison? Lighten up. I'm teasing you."

He smiled then, and I studied his deep-blue eyes, the way his shag of dark-blond hair teased his collar. He really was a cute guy. He said, "You should be this way more often."

"What way?"

"Laughing. Kidding around with your friends."

The way I used to be. "I'll take that under advisement."

"So, have you read it yet?"

The book on the dead thinkers.

"Not yet. But I will."

"You don't have to," he said. "It's not a requirement for hanging out with me."

"I know. It looks pretty challenging, though."

"It is, but it's totally worth it."

At the pool house a crowd of swimmers waited outside the gate. Harrison said, "Are you okay about seeing him?"

"Evan?" I ran a hand through my new haircut. "Might as well be. I can't avoid him for the rest of the season."

"Good attitude," Harrison said. "Listen. You want to ride this afternoon? A couple of the horses haven't had much exercise this week. They could use a workout."

"Sure, as long as we're back by four."

He waved and started for the stables. I used my key to unlock the rear door of the pool house. A whistle blew, the gate opened, and the swimmers streamed inside. The door opened, and Evan came in. He did a double take, checking out my new look. I pretended to be busy with paperwork. He dumped his stuff into his wire basket, coated his nose with sunblock, and helped himself to a soda from the machine, all the while scanning the pool from the open window.

Finally he said, "Hi."

"Hello."

"You changed your hair. And everything. You look fantastic!"

I flattened the empty shipping cartons. "Excuse me, please."

I headed for the trash bin out back. He rushed to open the door for me. "Look, I know I didn't handle things very well. I'm sorry for the way it turned out. I didn't mean—"

"Shouldn't you be out there on the lifeguard tower, protecting innocent lives?"

"I'm watching them. They're okay."

I shoved the cartons into the trash bin and headed back inside. Evan followed. "We still have to work together, Haley. It'll be best if we can forget what happened."

"Fine."

He ran his fingers through his hair. "Are you going to be like this for the rest of the summer?"

"Like what?"

"Stuck up. Angry. Barely talking to me. When you know how I feel about you."

I stared at him, openmouthed. "How you *feel* about me? Please."

"Look. You know how summer romances are. We'd have to break up at the end of the season anyway, right? I thought it would be best to get it over with before I fell even more in love with you."

Two weeks before, those words would have melted my very bones. Now I just laughed. "You wouldn't know love if it jumped up and bit you."

"That isn't true."

"You know what? You're right. You *are* in love. With Evan Cole."

Just then a skinny kid wearing Hawaiian-print swim trunks rushed inside. "Evan! Some guy stole my iPod and won't give it back. My mom will kill me!"

"I'm coming, Seth."

Evan followed him outside. I sat on the stool behind the counter, feeling shaky but also elated that I had faced Evan and survived.

People started coming in for ice cream and towels, and I was busy for the rest of my shift. I was refilling the ice machine when Byron arrived to relieve Evan.

Evan came inside and stuck out his hand. "Truce?"

"Whatever." I closed the top of the ice machine and set the empty pail beside the door.

He grinned. "Great!"

I propped the back door open and prepared to wheel the towel cart outside. Evan hurried past the counter. "Um, Haley? Would you help me with the newsletter again? I mean, you're so good at it, and you can write so fast! It takes me hours, and it still isn't as great as when you do it. I would really appreciate it."

"I'm sure you would, Evan. Especially since Mr. Porter thinks you're doing such a fantastic job."

"You're mad about *that*?" He shook his head. "I never figured you to be so small-minded."

"I have to go. I have a date."

"I heard you were hanging out with the cowpoke. He doesn't seem like your type."

"That just shows how little you really know about me." I grabbed the towel cart and headed for the laundry.

Chapter Twenty

Back in grade school my favorite teacher was Mrs. Brightman. Every morning of my third-grade year she stood outside the classroom door drinking coffee from a chipped TEACHERS HAVE CLASS mug and welcoming us to school. Her day-to-day wardrobe of slacks, sweaters, and denim jumpers worn over turtleneck tees was nothing special, but her collection of battery-powered, holiday-themed earrings was something else. She had jack-o'-lanterns for Halloween, snowmen for Christmas, and shamrocks for St. Patrick's Day, all of which glowed or twinkled. And Mrs. Brightman seemed to be everywhere: in the cafeteria at lunch, opening stubborn milk cartons; on the playground, refereeing games of dodgeball; after school, grading papers at her desk. I figured she lived at school, in a book-filled room on the second floor, near where the custodian stored his mops and pails.

One Thursday afternoon Mom and I saw Mrs. Brightman downtown, wheeling a grocery cart out of the A&P. I stared at her, totally stunned. Mrs. Brightman wasn't supposed to be there. The same surreal feeling came over me at the resort one steamy August morning, when I looked up from the lawn where I was hanging out with Nora and Frankie and saw Camilla Quinn in the office parking lot.

"Haley?" Nora pushed her sunglasses to the top of her head and peered into my face. "Are you okay?"

"It's her."

"Who?"

"Camilla. The one I told you about."

"You're not serious," Frankie said. "What is *she* doing here?"

"I don't know, but I'm not hanging around to find out."

Nora and I were spending the weekend at Frankie's. I was looking forward to catching some sun and having lunch. I'd decided to stop by the staff party after all before going back to Frankie's to listen to Harrison's radio show. The response to his music on KPQR had been so good that Rick Matheny had moved Harrison to Fridays at eight p.m., a better time slot. Now all I could think about was avoiding Camilla.

"Running away is the worst thing you can do." Frankie stood and brushed off the seat of her lime-green shorts. "If Camilla is checking in for a week's stay, you'll have to face her sometime."

"Not if I see her coming first."

Nora glanced at her watch. "Let's go somewhere else for lunch. There's probably not much left in the staff kitchen anyway."

The end of the season was fast approaching, and the chefs were trying to use up all their ingredients before the resort closed, a situation that had resulted in some unfortunate experiments best left to those with an adventurous palate.

"Good call." Frankie popped a stick of gum into her mouth. "I'm not really up for another round of beet and mushroom soup."

We headed for the parking lot, Frankie in the lead.

Nora said, "Haley, are you all set for movie night tomorrow?"

"I guess so. I can't wait to get it over with."

"Last movie of the season," Nora said. "The theater will be packed."

"*The Wizard of Oz* always draws a crowd," Frankie said, slowing as we climbed a rise. "The place will be crawling with little kids."

At least the crowd would make it harder for Camilla to spot me running around in my ridiculous lion getup. Maybe she wouldn't even recognize me. Then all I'd have to do would be to get through my shifts at the pool house. With any luck, by the next Saturday she'd be gone, and I'd be home free.

We reached the parking lot. Nora punched my arm. "Stop obsessing about Camilla. Let's just have fun."

We drove to Pinehurst for lunch, then headed back to

Frankie's house. Crystal Marie came running out to greet us, her tiny little feet scrabbling on the hardwood floor. She yipped and jumped until Frankie scooped her up and put her in a playpen with a couple of Milk-Bones and a chewed-up teddy bear. "Here you go, sweetie. Be a good girl and take a nap."

We went upstairs to Frankie's room and spent the rest of the afternoon talking and listening to B.B. King, Nina Simone, and Etta James, until Nora said, "Hey, Frankie? Call me shallow, but don't you have anything that was recorded in the last hundred years?"

She handed me a bottle of purple nail polish and stuck her bare feet in my lap. I uncapped it and started painting her toenails. Frankie popped another CD into the player. "If you had one chance at everything you wanted / would you, could you seize the day? / Would you, could you let it fall away? / That moment is now / Baby, please stay."

"They're pretty good," Nora said, bobbing her head to the beat.

"It's a new group called Looie," Frankie said. "They won a battle of the bands at the fair last year."

We listened to the rest of the CD. I got ready for the staff party. "We'll pick you up as soon as Mom gets back," Frankie said. Nora drove me to the pavilion. People milled around, talking and eating, reminiscing about the summer that was rapidly drawing to a close. Several guys were diving off the pier, seeing who could stay underwater the longest. The lights were on even though it wasn't yet dark. The deejay put the music on, and several couples started to dance. I thought about my first dance with Evan, when I'd been so crazy for him and so sure he loved me back.

"Haley."

I turned around. "Hi, Elaine."

"I just wanted to say I think you look great. I love your haircut."

"Thanks."

We watched the dancers for a minute.

"I've broken up with Evan. For the last time." She brushed her palms together like she was dusting them off. "We are so over."

"Um. Good?"

She laughed. "I thought you'd like to know. In case you want him back."

"He's not my type of person."

"How has your summer been otherwise?"

"Good," I said, realizing that it was actually true.

"Are you planning to work here next year?" Elaine asked. "I'm sure Mr. Porter will invite you back. You could work in the office, writing the newsletters."

Just then Annie strolled by with CJ. After the part she'd played in the whole Peyton drama, she hadn't had the nerve to talk to me.

"If you decide you want to, let me know," Elaine said. "I'll make sure you don't have to work with Evan."

"Thanks, I will."

She moved away. I filled a plate and nibbled on cheese pizza even though I was still pretty full from lunch. A few minutes later Evan showed up with a big-chested blond girl I'd never seen before, making a big deal of his entrance. I watched him kidding around with the guys, holding onto Blondie's hand, and I realized that the magic was gone. Evan Cole was just an ordinary guy with questionable values. I didn't know what I'd ever seen in him.

"There you are!" Nora said, raising her voice above the pulse of the music. "We should go pretty soon if we want to catch Harrison's show."

We stuck around long enough to schmooze with Mr. Porter, who shook our hands and gushed about what a great job everyone had done. As soon as he left, we rescued Frankie from an earnest conversation with the pimply-faced boy who ran the movie projection equipment, and drove back to her house.

Harrison's show was great. He sang a mix of songs by famous and not-so-famous bands, interspersed with his own material. His voice was deep and smooth, just right for radio. I let the music wash over me, remembering that warm afternoon when he'd said music was as much about feelings as sound, and that a person couldn't sing what he hadn't lived. Lying on Frankie's bed, I closed my eyes and concentrated on his voice, on the feeling pouring out of his songs, so I wouldn't have to think about Camilla out at the resort, a poisonous spider just lying in wait.

\||/

The next morning we piled into Nora's car and headed for work. Even though Mr. Porter had roped me into subbing for Merrie Matheson at the pool house on my day off, I was in a good mood, giddy with the knowledge that this was my last week at the resort. Frankie rode shotgun with Nora as usual; I shared the backseat with the huge box containing my lion costume. Frankie and Nora headed for the kitchen, and I hurried to the pool house, watching out for Camilla, my head shifting right and left like the bad guy in a crime movie, trying to elude the cops. I unlocked the back door and hurried though the towel count, keeping one eye on the crowd of swimmers gathering at the gate. Byron arrived and let them inside, then came in to grab a soda and some sunblock.

"Haley. What are you doing here?"

"Merrie's sick."

"Evan and I switched again today, in case you were wondering."

"I figured."

I checked the cash register and filled the freezer and the ice machine, my whole body on autopilot.

Byron helped himself to a cup of ice. "You okay? You seem out of it today."

"I'm just tired from the party last night."

"Yeah. It was fun. See you later."

Time slowed to a crawl as I waited for the end of my shift. Every time the door opened I held my breath, praying not to see Camilla, and for once it seemed that the universe paid attention to my desires. Two o'clock came, and I was safe. I met up with Nora and Frankie, and we drove to the country club and spent the rest of the afternoon lying in the sun.

When it was time to dress for movie night, Nora drove me back to the resort. I got into my Cowardly Lion costume and Frankie applied makeup to my face, giving me a triangular nose, whiskers, and exaggerated cat eyes.

"Wa-la!" She handed me a mirror and stood back to admire her handiwork. "You look so different your own mother wouldn't recognize you."

"Great. That's exactly the look I'm going for."

She grinned. "Don't worry. Nora and I will be right behind you."

We walked up the hill to the amphitheater. As Frankie had predicted, the place was packed with harried, sunburned parents and hordes of kids clutching bags of popcorn and cans of soda. Most of the staff were already in place, handing out programs and telling everyone to enjoy the movie. Harrison was stationed at the opposite end of the amphitheater. He waved, and I waved back. Annie and CJ were standing together near the popcorn machines, chatting with a couple of little kids. Behind me Nora and Frankie were handing out programs and helping people find empty spaces where they could set up their lawn chairs. Just as I was beginning to relax, I saw Camilla, in red shorts and a white crop top, pushing her father's wheelchair toward the entrance.

"There she is," I muttered to Frankie. "Hide me."

"Uh-oh." Frankie stepped in front of me as Camilla maneuvered the wheelchair along the uneven path. "Where's your bully repellent?"

I crouched down to talk to a little girl wearing a *Wizard*

of Oz T-shirt. Camilla walked past, and I breathed again. I watched her park her father's wheelchair and set the brake. A few people recognized Mr. Quinn. Soon his chair was surrounded, and Camilla was lost in the crowd.

"That was close," Nora said as the crowd continued streaming in.

We handed out more programs and helped a family with six kids find a place to sit. A couple of little girls carrying plush Toto look-alikes asked to have their picture taken with me. I knelt on the grass between them while their mom fiddled with her camera. The flash went off, and the girls scrambled away.

The projector lights came on, and the audience clapped. Phoebe, her face smeared with lime-green makeup, came toward me holding the hem of her Wicked Witch costume. "Haley! Isn't this totally lame? I feel like an idiot."

I was just about to answer her when another voice said, "Haley *Patterson*? Oh. My. God. It *is* you!"

I couldn't speak. I felt faint.

"Well, well," Camilla said, circling me like a boxer looking for an opening. "The *Cowardly* Lion. How apropos."

"Whoa," Frankie said. "Back off."

Camilla turned around. "Who are you?"

Nora said, "We're her friends."

Camilla laughed. "Haley the Ho actually has *friends*? Well, color me surprised."

"We're surprised too," Nora said calmly. "We thought your kind came out only on Halloween."

"What's that supposed to mean?"

"Just what it sounds like. The movie's starting. Take your seat."

"I'll take a seat when I feel like it."

Just then Camilla spotted Evan, and her whole expression changed. "Wow. That guy is smoking hot," she said, almost to herself. "I wonder if he's available."

Frankie's face lit up, and I could almost see one of those cartoon lightbulbs going on over her head signaling the arrival of a brilliant idea. She winked at me and Nora. "Isn't he something?" she said to Camilla. "That's our head lifeguard. If you think he's hot in jeans, you should see him in his Speedo."

Camilla just nodded, evidently rendered speechless by the mental image of Evan in tight swim trunks.

Frankie went on. "He's seeing someone, and unfortunately she's very possessive and just a wee bit crazy."

Nora bit her lip to keep from laughing. Frankie said, "However, if you'll apologize to Haley for your rude behavior, I'll arrange for you to meet him."

"I can get guys on my own. I don't need you to arrange anything."

"Suit yourself," Frankie said. "But if his girlfriend catches you talking to him, I can't be responsible for what she might do."

Nora nodded solemnly. "That last girl—what was her name? I forget. Anyway, it was such a shame. She was so beautiful until—"

Camilla rolled her eyes and folded her arms. "*Sorry!* Okay?"

I stood there in my stupid lion costume, totally stunned. I'd always known Camilla wasn't in danger of being mistaken for an intellectual, but I'd never before realized that she was so gullible.

Frankie said, "That's not the most heartfelt apology I've ever heard, but it's a start."

The music began, and another round of applause rippled across the darkening lawn as the black and white image of Dorothy and Toto filled the screen. Frankie turned to Camilla. "Wait here."

She made her way through the crowd, spoke to Evan while Dorothy's house tumbled through the sky, and returned just as Dorothy revived from the impact of the crash and opened the door to the Yellow Brick Road.

"Well?" Camilla demanded. "What did he say?"

"He thinks you're hot. He wants to meet you, too."

"I knew it!"

Frankie nodded. "He wants you to meet him at the falls."

Nora and I exchanged glances. Camilla had it coming, but the trail was dangerous, especially at night. I sent Frankie a warning look, which she ignored. "You know where it is, right?" She kept her voice low to avoid disturbing the movie patrons. "Follow the hiking trail past the fire pit and keep going to reach the overlook."

Camilla said, "I saw it on the map they gave us when we checked in. But what about Dad? I'll have to take him back to the cabin after the movie."

"You'll have time. Evan has to take his girlfriend home; then he'll drive back here and meet you at the falls."

Nora said, "Let's go, Haley. We're supposed to be circulating."

We sauntered through the crowd while Camilla hurried back to her dad. The three of us collapsed on the stone steps leading to the parking lot and watched the rest of the movie. On the screen Dorothy was discovering that the wizard didn't have any special powers after all.

"You are *insane*," I whispered to Frankie. "What if she goes up there and gets herself killed?"

"Relax. After the last big rainstorm, part of the trail washed out, and they closed it just past the fire pit. There's no way she can get to the falls. But she's not exactly the brightest bulb on the tree. She'll sit at the barricade half the night waiting for Evan."

Nora giggled. "It's perfect. But how did you get Evan to cooperate?"

"That's the beauty of it," Frankie said. "He doesn't suspect a thing. When she confronts him about standing her up, he'll be all 'what are you talking about?' and that will make her even madder. It's brilliant. It may be my most brilliant plan ever."

Nora said, "Here comes Harrison," and I saw his tiny penlight flickering in the dark. He plopped down next to me and grinned. "Nice outfit."

"Thanks. I like yours, too."

Tonight's T-shirt featured a portrait of the president with a cartoon bubble coming out of his mouth: "IS OUR CHILDREN LEARNING?"

We watched the final minutes of the movie. When it

ended Frankie said, "It's still early. Let's go down to the pavilion for a while."

"I'm in," Nora said. "Anything is better than going home and listening to my sisters fighting. Those two are in serious need of anger-management classes."

"Come with us," Frankie said to Harrison. "I'll grab a cooler and we'll hang out and talk."

I saw what Frankie was up to. In order to get back to her cabin from the hiking trail, Camilla would have to pass right by the pavilion. Frankie wanted to make sure Camilla would have an audience.

Harrison said, "I guess I could come by for a while." Breaking his no-party rule.

Nora went with me to help me change out of my lion costume and scrub off my makeup. Frankie wandered through the crowd, rounding up others for our impromptu party. By the time Nora and I arrived at the pavilion, a dozen or so staffers were there, drinking sodas from Frankie's cooler and listening to a boom box. Byron and Evan were sitting atop a picnic table talking. Phoebe and Elaine were sitting on the pier with their diet sodas, dragging their bare feet in the water. They waved to me, and I waved back, my eyes scanning the crowd for Harrison. Finally I saw him talking to Frankie. I was sure she was clueing him in to her plot, and the realization filled me with shame all over again. On the outside I was the new and improved Haley, with a cool haircut and the latest in makeup. On the inside, where it mattered most, I was the same old don't-make-waves coward.

After a few minutes Nora left to join Phoebe and Elaine. Harrison handed me a diet soda. "I never got a chance to ask if you caught my last show."

"Are you kidding? I wouldn't miss it for anything. I liked every song you played."

"I picked stuff I thought you'd like."

Another song blared through the boom box. Byron jumped up and asked Nora to dance. Annie paired off with CJ. Elaine left the pier and asked one of the golf guys to dance, pointedly ignoring Evan, who promptly swept Frankie into his arms without waiting for an invitation. Which was a perfect pairing, since Frankie was in zero danger of falling for him.

"Dance with me," Harrison said.

He wrapped his arms around my waist, drawing me close. It wasn't awkward, like dancing with someone I wanted to impress; it was totally natural, as if we had danced together forever, and all at once I got that strange, jumpy feeling deep in the pit of my stomach. Harrison said, "I've been thinking."

"You're always thinking."

He laughed. "I'm just trying to figure out where I fit in the world."

"Everybody worries about fitting in, only they don't read metaphysics to try to figure it out."

"So does that make me weird, or what?"

"It makes you interesting."

"Then I'm not boring you. Good to know. Because I'm enrolling at Harwood College in the fall."

"Harwood is only a couple of hours from Ridgeview!"

"An added bonus. It's really small, but they have a great music department, and they're going to let me enroll as a noncredit student until I can complete all the applications. The head of the department is a master of composition. I could learn *everything* from him, Haley! And I could visit you sometimes." He paused. "If you want."

Until that very second I hadn't thought at all about seeing Harrison after the summer ended. I figured he'd pack up his van and his guitar and move on to some other town, catching odd jobs and writing songs while he searched for his place in the cosmos. Now I couldn't think of anything I wanted more than to have this boy in my life.

In the shadows beneath the twinkling pavilion lights, as the last strains of the song faded away, Harrison bent his head and kissed me, and I felt like the clueless girl in a romantic comedy who suddenly realizes that the boy next door, the loyal friend who has seen her at her absolute worst, is the One who can bring her love and happiness.

As another song began, Nora and Frankie hurried over. Frankie pointed to a bright beam of light shining through the trees. "Here comes Camilla."

Superdiva emerged from the darkness with her perfect hair all tangled, her shoes caked with mud, and her tight red shorts sporting a huge tear that exposed her white lace underwear.

Frankie yelled, "Camilla Quinn! Is that you?"

Camilla stomped over to the pavilion, her eyes narrowed in anger. She shoved her way through the knot of people until she was standing nose to nose with Evan. "You slime bucket!"

"What?" Evan frowned, and Frankie winked at me, obviously enjoying the fact that everything was working out just the way she'd planned it.

"You stood me up and almost got me killed!"

"I don't know what you're talking about," Evan said, as if Frankie had handed him a script. He looked so genuinely confused that I felt sorry for him. Almost.

"You *said* you'd meet me at the falls, only the trail was closed, so then I tried to climb over the barrier, only it was too tall, and I tore my clothes, and do you have any *idea* how much I paid for these shoes?"

Evan stared at her. "I never heard of you before in my life. You are a nutcase!"

Everybody laughed, and Camilla's face turned bright red.

"Somebody may have promised to meet you at the falls," Evan said, "but it wasn't me." He turned to Byron. "Let's get out of here."

Camilla watched them go, then spun back around to Frankie. "You! You set this whole thing up just to embarrass me!"

"How does it feel?" Nora put in. "Being singled out and humiliated in front of people?"

Camilla turned on me then. "Don't think for one minute that I don't realize you are the one who put them up to this, Haley. So you just go right on and have your fun. Because once we get back home, I'll make sure you pay."

She pushed her tangled hair out of her eyes. "If you think last spring was bad, you just wait. I'll make your miserable excuse for a life ten times worse. You know I can, and I will."

Everything around me suddenly seemed too quiet. The boom box had shut itself off after the last CD played; out on the highway the traffic noise faded to a hum. Water lapped against the pier. Frankie and Nora were standing close behind me. Harrison's shoulder pressed mine. Something inside me shifted, a gathering up of the pieces of myself that I thought had been chipped away forever.

"No," I said slowly. "I don't think so."

"You don't *think* so?" Camilla tossed her head. "You make me laugh."

"Go ahead. See who laughs last."

Camilla's shoes squished as she stepped back, her eyes darting from me to Nora, Frankie, Harrison, and back again. "What are you talking about?"

Harrison found my hand in the darkness and held on tight.

I looked Camilla in the eye. "Color you busted."

After that night everything happened at warp speed. A small army of people arrived to help close the resort for the season. Cleaning crews swarmed over the guest cabins like ants, the pool service company drained the pool and rolled the cover into place, and, mercifully, CJ and the chef ran out of beets and mushrooms.

Frankie organized a girls' night at her house, and I spent the night scarfing down pizza with her, Nora, Melanie, and Phoebe. Dad called. He and Mom were home, but he was heading west with Peyton, who had liked California so much he'd decided to enroll at UCLA. Aunt Bitsy was drafted to drive me back to Ridgeview.

"Road trip!" she crowed, when Dad asked her about it. "We'll take our time, Haley, and I'll show you the campus where I went to college. You'll love it."

On my last night in Copper Springs, Aunt B agreed to let me stay out until midnight. Harrison and I took another picnic up to the Eagle Mountain lookout and spent the whole time talking about anything and everything.

"Peyton is the big achiever in our family," I said. "He's good at everything, and he's never afraid to rebel against anything he doesn't like. I'm afraid of speaking up, afraid of disappointing people."

"Hey, a little rebellion is a good thing," Harrison said. "Don't worry about talking to your folks. They're stronger than you think. They can take it."

He picked up his guitar and played a song I hadn't heard before.

"That's pretty. What's it called?"

"Haven't finished it yet." He grinned. "When I do, though, you'll be the first to know."

We packed up and drove home along the quiet streets. At Back in Thyme a cat-shaped lamp lit the window. The fountain in the park burbled quietly; the carousel was still. At the main intersection the traffic light blinked on and off. We drove without talking until Harrison stopped in our driveway. Crickets sang in the grass. An old Beatles tune played on the radio.

"I guess this is it." My voice wobbled. Already I was missing Harrison more than I'd ever imagined I could.

He kissed me, his hand on the back of my neck. "I'll see you soon, okay?"

It was more than okay. It was fantabulous. I hugged him one last time and got out of the van. Harrison grinned at me through the open window. "Harwood, here I come!"

I watched until the van's taillights disappeared at the bottom of the hill.

Chapter Twenty-One

Imagination often magnifies a person's fears into something much worse than reality, as I discovered when I finally sat down with my parents to explain everything I'd gone through last spring. I was afraid they'd have a bad opinion of me, or ground me for lying to them, but a couple of days after my road trip home with Aunt B I got up the courage to tell them the whole story, including, as embarrassing as it was, the day I'd discovered my locker plastered with condoms.

Mom hugged me and cried, and when I told them about the e-mail, things got serious. Dad retrieved it off the hard drive, and the next week he drove me to the lawyers' office to give my deposition. I repeated my story, and Dad gave them a copy of the e-mail.

After I finished going over the details about a gazillion

times, the lady lawyer said I'd been very helpful indeed, thanked me for coming, and told me to wait outside while they finished talking to Dad.

I was standing in the hallway when a girl in jeans and a yellow tank top left her chair near the elevators and made her way over to me. As she got closer, I could see an angry red seam running from just above her eye to the top of her head. Her hair looked like it had been all shaved off and was just now growing back, short and downy like fuzz on a new chick.

"Are you Haley Patterson?" she asked.

"Yeah. You must be Angie."

She ran her hand over her head. "An easy guess."

We stood there awkwardly for a minute. A couple of lawyer types headed for the elevator, talking about some baseball game. Then Angie said, "My dad said you were coming in today. I was hoping to see you, to thank you for coming forward. I know it was hard, and you really didn't have to."

"Yeah, I did. Does your head hurt?"

"Not much now. It did at first." Her eyes filled with tears. "The doctors say the scar will fade as I get older. They say eventually I'll hardly notice it all."

"That's good."

"But what am I supposed to do in the meantime? School starts next week, and I look like a total freak."

"Just act confident," I said. "It'll be okay."

On the way home Dad stopped at the paper to sign off on the next day's edition, and I spent the time window-shopping along Commerce Street. I was studying a display of sweaters in a boutique next to a jewelry store when Camilla emerged, carrying two shopping bags.

A month before, I would have walked away, but now I stood firm, claiming my space on the sidewalk.

"There she is, the spineless wonder," Camilla said. "So, do you feel better now that you've spilled your guts to those lawyers?"

"Yeah, as a matter of fact, I do."

She shook her head. "Boy, Patterson, I never figured you for such a poor sport. All that stuff at school last spring? I was just messing with your head 'cause I was mad that you ratted me out and Dad canceled my trip to New York. And now you've made a huge court case out of it."

"Oh, you were just messing with my head. What you did was way beyond that, and you know it. You turned the entire school against me."

"The entire school? Don't flatter yourself. You're just not that important."

She shifted her shopping bags to her other arm. "You know what else really stinks? My dad is all stressed out over this thing. You should be ashamed for causing so much worry to a man in a wheelchair."

"If you want someone to blame for stressing out your dad, go look in the mirror," I shot back. Just then Dad came out of the *Record* office. "I have to go."

School started. The first few days of sophomore year passed in a blur of new schedules, new teachers, and new gossip, some of it directed at me. Gracie and a couple of Camilla's other minions blamed me for getting Camilla in trouble, but girls who had been my friends before were at least talking to me again. Angie's case was settled out of court, and the week after that Camilla transferred to Jefferson High. Good news.

Bad news: Vanessa didn't come back to Ridgeview for our sophomore year. Her mom took a new job in London, and Vanessa stayed in New Jersey with Daddy-o. But at least he hadn't married Irene. Vanessa enrolled in an arts magnet school where she could paint and throw clay to her heart's content, and she was totally besotted with Josh, the guy she'd met at science camp. The good thing was, Josh was totally into Vanessa, too.

"Jersey is the pits, but at least I'll get a better quality of Christmas presents now," Vanessa said during one of our frequent phone calls.

I switched the phone to my other ear and looked out my window. Peyton was back from UCLA for homecoming weekend at Ridgeview. He and some of his friends from high school were standing in our yard, drinking from oversize soda cups and talking over old times. Peyton had offered to escort me to the homecoming dance, but honestly, I didn't want to go. Angie had said she might stop by later, Harrison was going to be on the radio, and I was working on my new column for the *Raider Review*. The Supreme Court in Washington, D.C., was about to decide another case involving school newspapers and free speech, and I had plenty to say about censorship and why stifling a person's voice is generally a bad idea.

"Are you listening to me, Haley?" Vanessa asked. "We're talking major loot here."

"Yeah," I said, remembering all the stuff I'd received for my birthday while Mom and Dad were in England. "The old guilt factor is pretty powerful."

She laughed. "Speaking of guilt, did Camilla ever admit what she did to you and Hannah?"

"I don't know. I heard that her transfer to Jefferson was part of the court settlement, but the records were sealed. Even Dad couldn't get much out of the two lawyers he interviewed for the paper. I'd love to know what Camilla said when they showed her that e-mail, but the important thing is, she's out of here."

"Stick a fork in her—she's done!" Vanessa crowed. "I'm proud of you, Haley."

"Thanks."

"So what's with you and Suzanne?"

"It's weird. I see her in the halls. She's in my third-period history class, but we don't really talk. She seems lost without Camilla."

"Now that's what's truly weird," Vanessa said. "Because Suzanne never really belonged with that bunch."

It was true. Camilla never picked the prettiest or most talented girls for her inner circle; she preferred girls who wouldn't outshine her. Suzanne, who was both beautiful and whip-smart, never really fit the mold. Plus, Camilla was the kind of person who could make a simple compliment like "cute shoes" sound like an insult. Suzanne wasn't like that.

"Maybe it's too late for us to be friends again," I said.

"She's probably ashamed of the way she treated you," Vanessa said. "I know I am. I should have tried harder to defend you last year. I'm sorry I didn't."

"I hated you for it," I admitted. "But I understand why you didn't."

"No backbone," Vanessa said. "But I'm trying to grow one in case I need it for the future."

We laughed, and then she said, "Oops, there's Josh. Talk to you soon. Bye!"

I hung up the phone, turned my laptop off, stretched out on my bed, and tuned the radio to my favorite station. A cool evening breeze blew through my open window, bringing with it the sounds of Saturday night traffic and the faint smell of burning leaves.

"Hello again, everyone," said the radio announcer. "It's eight p.m., and this is Rege Chapman, broadcasting live from the campus of Harwood College. Hey, you probably heard KHCR radio is sponsoring a series of live performances from around the country this fall, showcasing the best new talent in America, and believe me, we're gonna be bringing you great music all semester long. That'll take the sting out of midterm exams, right? Okay, so listen, we're gonna kick things off tonight with a young man who almost didn't make it to Harwood this fall, Harrison Gray. Hey man, whassup?"

"Hi," Harrison said. "It's great to be here."

"We'll be right back with Harrison Gray after these words from our sponsors," the announcer said. "Grab a cool one while you're waiting, 'cause I can guarantee, this boy's music is hot, hot, hot!"

I didn't grab a cool one. I scooted closer to the radio so I wouldn't miss a single note of Harrison's song. Since enrolling at Harwood he'd been too busy to visit Ridgeview, but we IMed each other late at night, when the quiet and the darkness made it seem like we were the only two people on the planet who were still awake. Harrison had abandoned the song he'd been working on over the summer, but he told me he'd finished a new pop/country song and to be sure to tune in so I wouldn't miss it.

"And we're back," Rege Chapman said, "talkin' with Harrison Gray, live from the campus of Harwood College. So, Harrison, are you ready to rock?"

"Ready." In the background I could hear Harrison settling his guitar into place, softly strumming the strings. "Here's a song inspired by a special girl who shared the summer with me. Haley, if you're out there listening, this one's for you.

> *"Christmas morning I was six years old*
> *Santa left me a brand-new bike*
> *With shiny silver handlebars*
> *And bright red racing stripes*
> *Out on the street, no training wheels*
> *And the road still slick with snow*
> *I held my breath, I held on tight*
> *And said, 'Daddy, don't let go.'*

"Don't let go, keep holding on.
Don't look back, don't look down.
Just keep going strong.

"Summertime up in Copper Springs
I met a girl who had paid the cost
Of shattered friendships and shattered dreams
She was feeling lost
I said I'm no expert at living life
There's plenty I still don't know
But when you're talkin' about your hopes
  and dreams
Girl, you can't let go."

I sang the refrain along with Harrison, and by the time the song ended, I was laughing and crying all at once. Nobody had ever written a song for me before. Call it karma, call it some kind of cosmic benevolence—somehow Harrison's music erased the last vestiges of my bad year, and I felt ready to move forward into the future I imagined.

Later, lying in bed, I thought about Suzanne and Vanessa, about Frankie and Nora and how they had taken me under their wings and befriended me at a time when I distrusted everybody, including myself. I thought of how Peyton had morphed into superbro, calling me all the way from California just to see how sophomore year was going (just splendidly, thank you very much), then showing up for the homecoming festivities because he knew it was a big deal to me.

And Harrison, the boy who'd shown me the way it's supposed to be when a girl and a guy are totally into each other. Like he said in his song, I'm no expert, but I've decided that maybe life is just one big cycle of finding people and letting them go, and the trick is in holding on to the ones who will stand by you no matter what—if only you are brave enough to open your heart and let them in.

Author's Note

If you or someone you know is being harassed, threatened, or physically harmed, you are not alone. Experts say that each year almost six million teens are involved in some type of bullying. Maybe it's through rumors, gossip, or threats that arrive in e-mail or by text message. Maybe it's through stealing or damaging of personal belongings. Maybe it's through tripping, punching, or hitting someone when no one is looking. However it happens, it's wrong, and help is available. To find out how to get help for yourself or for others, go to www.safeyouth.org and follow the "teen" links. Or call the National Youth Violence Prevention Resource Center at 1-866-safeyouth (1-866-723-3968).

By taking a stand and lending a hand, you can be a big part of the solution.